Holly Webb

The Girl of Glass

ORCHARD

ORCHARD BOOKS

First published in Great Britain in 2017 by The Watts Publishing Group

1 3 5 7 9 10 8 6 4 2

Text copyright © Holly Webb, 2017

The moral right of the author has been asserted.

A CIP catalogue record for this book is available from the British Library.

ISBN 978 1 40832 768 5

Typeset in Adobe Caslon by Avon DataSet Ltd, Bidford-on-Avon, Warwickshire

Printed and bound in Great Britain by CPI Group (UK) Ltd, Croydon, CR0 4YY

The paper and board used in this book are made from
wood from responsible sources.

Orchard Books
An imprint of Hachette Children's Group
Part of The Watts Publishing Group Limited
Carmelite House
50 Victoria Embankment
London EC4Y 0DZ

An Hachette UK Company
www.hachette.co.uk

www.hachettechildrens.co.uk

For Eva and Bron to read together

CHAPTER ONE

'MARIANA! COME OUT OF THERE!'

Mariana whirled around guiltily. Her stepmother was standing at the door of the workshop, hissing at her. She had lingered – she should have known that Mama would have noticed. She hurried to the doorway, hearing the apprentices sniggering behind her. She risked a quick glance over her shoulder to scowl and cross her eyes at Rafa and Giorgio, but they were already back stoking the furnace and didn't see her.

'Stop that!' Mariana's stepmother caught her by the wrist and yanked her out of the workshop. 'What were you doing in the workshop, you stupid girl?'

'I only wanted to watch,' Mariana muttered. 'I wanted to see Papa. I wasn't doing anything wrong.'

'I need you helping in the shop.'

'Dusting!' Mariana twisted in her stepmother's grip, trying to pull her arm away. 'Again?' Then she caught the angry glitter in Mama's eyes and subsided, not wanting a slap.

'You can go into the city for me, then. I've a list – go down to the boats and find someone to take you over.'

Mariana nodded, swallowing a sigh. A trip across the lagoon to Venice was better than hours dusting and polishing the glittering glass vessels and ornaments stacked in the windows of the shop. But she knew what would be on the list. More expensive, useless spells. More incredible cure-alls that her stepmother had heard whispered about in the market. More promises.

None of it would work. Mariana and her father still hoped, of course. They hadn't given up, they never would. But for them it was a faint chance and nothing else, a tiny wisp of hope at the back of their minds. Mariana's stepmother blazed with certainty. Mariana suspected that it was because she couldn't allow herself not to believe. If she once admitted that Elizabetta might not recover, she would collapse, like a puppet with slashed strings.

It had been so subtle at first – Eliza had been such a healthy baby, big, with honey-brown curly hair and the clear skin and pink cheeks of an expensive wax doll. Mariana had been six when her little half-sister was born, and for a few months, she and her stepmother had united in adoration of the tiny girl. Eliza had been dressed like a little princess. The Vetrario Galdini was one of the best glassmaking workshops on the island, so Bianca Galdini could afford silk and lace dresses for her baby. But Eliza had been less than a year old when she started to sicken. The delicious plumpness of her cheeks wasted away, and though she grew, she was smaller than all the other children, slower to crawl, and then to walk. She scurried after the others, chattering like a little parrot, until she ran out of breath. Then Mariana or one of the older boys would scoop her up, carrying her piggyback while she wheezed and squeaked with joy.

Eliza was four years old now, but a stranger giving her a chance look would assume that she was a toddler, two or three at the most. Then they would see the waxy pallor of her skin, the strange flush of her cheeks when she tried to run with the others, the way she pressed her hands wearily against her chest. She spent much of her days curled on a sofa in the corner of the shop, playing with her dolls, and the glass trinkets her father conjured up to entertain her. Visitors to the shop would smile at her at first, the sweet baby, and then they would hear the catch in her breath, and note the thin little fingers combing through the dolls' hair, and look away uncomfortably.

'What is it this time?' Mariana muttered. She

dropped her eyes as her stepmother glanced up from her money pouch with a sharp look. 'I mean, where do you want me to go?'

'Can I go too?'

'Little Eliza! I thought you were asleep!' Mariana's stepmother thrust the pouch of coins at her, and hurried over to the corner of the shop, fussing at the fine wool blankets that were swathed around her daughter. 'Rest, dearest. You shall have a few spoonfuls of soup later, and then I'll carry you out to watch the seagulls. Mariana is going to the city, to find a tonic to help you breathe a little better, darling.'

'Please can't I go too? I'd like to see the shops. Won't you take me with you, Mariana?' The little girl reached out to Mariana, stretching out her claw-like fingers.

Mariana leaned over the arm of the sofa and smiled at her little sister. 'I wish I could take you, sweetness. But it's a long way, and in a little cockleshell boat, I expect. Probably that battered old thing of Leo's. It'll take an hour at least. And it's so chilly out on the water. You rest like Mama says, and I'll bring back the medicine.'

Eliza struggled to sit up straighter, as if she wanted to argue, but then the colour seemed to leach out of her face, and her lips looked tinged with blue. She swallowed, gulping air, and then glared sternly at her sister. 'You have to tell them to make it taste nice! The last one was horrid. It burned my throat.'

'I'll tell them,' Mariana promised.

'Here.' Her stepmother pressed a tiny scrap of paper into her hand. 'Signor Nesso's shop, on St Mark's Square.'

Mariana sucked in her breath with a hiss – St Mark's Square was the most expensive place in the city. Even though the workshop was doing so well, Mariana and her stepmother still never shopped there. It was a place for courtiers, for nobles, for those who did not need to work. A spell from a magic shop on the square would cost twice as much as one from anywhere else.

'You don't think your sister's worth it?' her stepmother snarled, rounding on her. Mariana stepped back hurriedly.

'I only meant—'

'Just go!'

Mariana sighed, and waved to Eliza. But her little sister didn't wave back – she was wriggling as her mother wrapped her tighter in the blankets. Mariana darted up the back stairs to fetch her hooded cloak from her bedroom, and then let herself out through the yard at the back of the shop, so as not to end up arguing with her stepmother again. Bianca had loved her once, Mariana knew she had. They'd adored Eliza together, when she was still well. Sometimes that closeness seemed still to be there, especially on the days when Eliza was a little stronger, or in the evenings, when she was peacefully sleeping upstairs. But when Eliza struggled to breathe, and couldn't move from the sofa, every step Mariana took seemed to infuriate her stepmother. Why should Mariana be so alive, when her own baby was slipping away?

Mariana knew that it was only because Mama was so worried about Eliza, but they didn't seem to be able to stay in the same room for five minutes without snapping and snarling now.

She slipped out of the little side passage on to the Fondamenta, the wide quay running down the side of the canal, lined with a thicket of tall mooring posts. Crowds of little boats were tied up all along the bank, several of them with their owners dozing in the sun, curled up half under the canvas covers.

'Leo!'

One of the smallest boats, a fragile-looking thing moored to a disintegrating wooden stump, rocked violently as the boy inside it woke up. 'What? Oh, it's you.'

Mariana crouched down at the edge of the stone quay. 'Leo, could you take me to the city? Close to Piazza San Marco? I know it's the wrong side of the city from here, but please… Or do you know anyone else who's going over? I'm on an errand for my stepmother.'

'Again?' The boy sat up, yawning. 'Didn't she send you out searching for some amulet just a few days ago?'

Mariana scowled. 'Yes, again. The amulet didn't work – of course it didn't. It was just a pretty purple stone. My father's apprentices could make more convincing amulets out of bits of spoiled glass. I might even suggest it to them, they could earn some money.'

'Didn't it do *anything*?' Leo pulled back the canvas cover and stuffed it into the little locker in the bows. He dusted the rough wooden bench in front of it with his hand, and bowed mockingly to Mariana.

'It sparkled a bit when Mama gave it to Eliza to hold,' Mariana said distractedly, as she scrambled from the quay into the boat. 'But that was all.'

'What did she say? She didn't send you back to the pedlar to complain?'

Mariana shook her head. 'You know what she's like. She's scared of magic. She'd never dare. All the cures, she thinks they're real, it's just that she hasn't found the right one for Eliza. She'll never stop. She thought all the sparkling meant that it was a most powerful enchantment.'

'Mmm.' Leo grunted. 'A glamour. Like brightening up the eyes on a fish that's past its best. Not that I'd ever do that.' He busied himself fussing over the mooring rope.

Mariana eyed him narrowly. 'Well, you'd better not sell one of those to me, anyway.'

'I wouldn't dare,' he muttered back. 'Who's doing who a favour, Signorina?'

'I can pay!'

'I didn't ask you to!' He glared at her, his face reddening, and Mariana sighed, and patted his hand on the oar.

'I'm sorry. I didn't mean that...'

She shouldn't have said it – they had been friends since they were small, too small to understand that she was the daughter of a prominent glassmaker, one whose glass was made even more strange and expensive by the magic he breathed into it. Leo's mother was a widow, who scraped a living mending clothes, for

Mariana's family among others. As soon as Leo was strong enough to handle his father's boat, he had gone out fishing each morning. He'd inherited his father's small magic, coaxing the fish into his nets and lobsters into his pots. Leo sold his catch wherever he could, often to the kitchens of the great Venice palazzos, but even with the money from the fish, he was still a great deal poorer than little Signorina Galdini.

'I brought you a bag of honey drops to say thank you,' she murmured, pulling them out of the pocket of her cloak. Leo didn't ever have the money spare for sweet things, and he loved them, far more than she did.

His eyes brightened, and he forgot to be offended. 'A bagful! That'll last me for a month, Mariana!' He grinned at her. 'That's worth the trip all round the city. And your passage back as well, if you want. Will you be long, finding whatever spell it is she wants this time?'

Mariana looked sideways. 'Well… No. Probably not. But I might tell Mama it took longer, if you see what I mean.'

He snorted. 'She won't believe you. Not if you go off exploring for hours again.'

'I'll just tell her they had to brew more of whatever this stuff is.' Mariana shrugged. 'It might even be true.'

'I've got people to see in the city. I'll come back for you, when you've finished nosing around the artists' workshops, and the maskmakers. Just don't get yourself covered in paint, or she'll know where you've been.'

'Thank you, *mother*.' Mariana rolled her eyes, but she was smiling. Venice was full of painters and sculptors, maskmakers and jewellers. Shop after shop filled with every kind of craft, most of them shaped with magic as well as skill. Mariana loved wandering there. She was surrounded by magic at home at the glassmaker's shop, but she was never allowed so much as to touch a blowpipe. Her father was old-fashioned that way. Traditional. No girls were glassmakers, it just wasn't the way; however much his daughter pleaded, he knew that it was so. Mariana ached to use the magic that she was sure she could feel inside her – but she was starting to understand that in Murano, that would never happen.

They gossiped idly for the rest of the journey, Mariana leaning over the side of the boat to peer into the greenish-brown depths of the lagoon. Dark shapes followed the boat, the fish wallowing up from the seabed, called by Leo's strange hunting magic. Every so often, she saw him flick his fingers on the oars, dismissing the confused creatures back to safer, deeper waters.

The city glittered in the autumn sunlight as they drew closer. Mariana caught her breath as the domes and towers grew taller, rising out of the water like some fantastical jewel. Murano was pretty, with all the houses painted in bright colours, and the boats bobbing at the jetties, but it wasn't grand like the city. It was a place of glassmakers and fishermen, friendly and bustling. Mariana loved the drama of the great palazzos and churches that crowded along the canals in Venice itself. Around every corner was another gorgeous marble frontage, carved and gilded, with nobles in absurdly perfect clothes dancing and feasting inside. The city was like a fairy tale – even the grubby back alleys only added to the strange glamour of the place.

Leo tied up at a long jetty out in front of Duchess Olivia's palace. 'I'll be rowing back before it gets dark,' he said, handing Mariana out on to the jetty. 'Don't be late.'

'I promise.' She huddled her cloak around her shoulders against the wind and hurried away, leaving Leo staring after her.

The scrap of paper said that Signor Nesso's shop was on the Piazza San Marco, but not exactly where. Mariana stood in the middle of the huge square with her back to the cathedral, peering uncertainly into the colonnades of shops. The piazza hummed around her, full of beautifully dressed nobles, either on their way to the church or the palace, or simply out to be seen, parading their fine clothes on this sunny afternoon.

A flock of tiny golden birds suddenly appeared from one of the archways that ran along the sides of the square, and Mariana smiled. The little creatures went spiralling up into the sky, singing in sweet, unearthly voices. They were a spell, she was almost sure. They would probably disappear once they were half a mile from their master. They were an advertisement – a very good one, judging by the admiring glances and cooed compliments from the crowds all around her. Mariana began to weave her way through the knots of people, making for the stone archway the birds had fluttered from. She paused at the line of pillars, looking into the shaded portico. She hadn't expected to be nervous – she had been to so many of these places now, on the hunt for a cure. But the archway looked dark against the glittering sunlit marble of the square. There was a faint, musky smell of magic, and the singing of the golden birds was still swooping in and out of the chattering crowd. The backs of her palms itched, and a cold sheen of sweat started up around her hairline.

She wanted desperately to walk into the shop – to see what was in there, to feel herself surrounded by magic, and magical things. But at the same time she could hardly bring herself to move.

'It's for Eliza,' Mariana whispered to herself, pushing her foot over the line of shadow, and shivering. 'This time it might even work.' She could feel the magic glowing in the stones of the walls, shimmering in the air. She could feel it calling to her, and something inside her rising up to answer. Surely magic so strong must be able to help mend her little sister?

In the cool dimness under the arches, she found a shop that looked surprisingly like her father's. Shelf after shelf was lined with glass bottles and stoppered porcelain jars. It was a cross between her father's shop and the provision merchant where she went with her stepmother sometimes. There were even sacks in neat rows around the walls, though Mariana suspected they were not filled with rice and dried beans. The hope inside her flattened. It was only a shop, after all. It was meant for making money. The spells would be pretty toys, like the others that her stepmother had bought.

'Yes, Signorina?'

Mariana jumped. She hadn't seen the man approach – he seemed just to have appeared out of the shadowy curtains at the back of the shop, without moving. She bobbed a neat curtsey – it would certainly do no harm to be polite, even if she suspected he couldn't help.

'I might be able to.'

Mariana stared at him, her mouth dropping open a little. Then she snapped it shut, and scowled. 'That's just as rude as eavesdropping on a conversation that you weren't meant to hear,' she announced frostily.

'Something I'm sure you *never* do,' the old man agreed, smiling at her. 'But sometimes, Signorina, one can't help but eavesdrop. If your mother and father are having an argument outside your bedroom door, for example.'

'But I wasn't—'

'Believe me, my dear, you were thinking uncommonly loud.'

'Oh…' Mariana eyed him sideways, still a little suspicious. Still, if he could read minds, he was truly magical in one way at least. Perhaps the magic really was as strong as she had thought, and his spells would be better than the others. She dropped another curtsey, wanting to begin again. 'Good morning, Signor. My stepmother sent me, to ask if you have any potions that might cure my little sister. She heard of a tonic that you gave one of our neighbour's children, I think. It cured his headaches.'

'Your sister doesn't have headaches, though, does she…?' the old man murmured, coming a little further out into the shop. His black velvet robes shifted around him. Shadows – that was all it had been. His black robes had sunk into the darkness of the curtains. It wasn't some magical appearance. 'You don't believe that any spell of mine – or anyone's – could mend her. Why?'

Mariana swallowed, and felt tears burn at the backs

of her eyes. 'She's been ill ever since she was little. But now she's getting worse, all the time. She finds it hard to breathe, and she can't walk alone any more. She's weaker every day, I think. I looked at her this morning, when I was helping her to dress, and she's so thin and pale. It – it was almost as if I could see through her skin. I hadn't noticed the change.' She looked at the old man, wondering how to explain. It didn't make sense, even to her. 'I suppose because I see Eliza all the time, and she's just been a tiny bit worse every day, I haven't realised how ill she is. Today I saw, properly… It was as if I looked at her for the first time in ages.'

The old man – Signor Nesso, the shop's owner, Mariana assumed – gave a sigh. He pulled two stools out from under a shelf and sat down, patting the other stool to tell Mariana to sit too. 'I understand, child. My poor wife failed in much the same way, a few years back.' He shook his head gently, watching Mariana's stricken eyes. 'No. I couldn't cure her either.'

'You cured Nico,' Mariana whispered. 'I saw him yesterday – playing about on the quay with his brothers. He looked well.'

'I gave his mother a mild sleeping draught for him, to ease the pain and let him rest. The attack passed on its own.'

'That isn't what Nico's mother said.' Mariana stared at him stubbornly, as if she could make him change his story, if she only argued enough. Even though she'd called her errand a waste of time, there had been that little seed of hope after all, deep down inside her. 'She said it was a miracle.'

'Everyone wants to believe in magic.'

'But you're a magician! You read my mind, you're real!'

'There are some things even magic can't mend, child. I'm so sorry. If your sister is weakening as you say she is, I can brew spells to ease her breathing, or to make her sleep, to give her sweet dreams, even. But I can't give her life back by magic.'

'There are all those stories, about wishes, and – and

girls waking up from glass coffins, and spells that can do everything! So why can't anyone help my sister?' Mariana whispered.

'If there's something deeply wrong with her, something that wasn't caused by magic in the first place, then it can't be cured by magic,' the old man explained. 'There are some spells…' He sighed. 'Not all magic is kind. It can be dangerous. Cruel, even. There could be ways to make your sister better, for a few weeks or months, but only by hurting someone else. Do you see?'

Mariana nodded. 'I'm not asking for that.'

'And even if you were, I would say no.' The old man's eyes glittered angrily in the dim light of the shop, and Mariana drew back a little, suddenly frightened.

'I know you weren't, child. Don't be afraid.'

'Do people often ask you to cast those sorts of spells?'

'More often than you would hope. But that's not something that you should be worrying about. Shall I brew you something for your sister?'

Mariana sighed. 'Could you make it taste nice? I know it shouldn't matter, but she did say the last tonic she had was horrible. Mama will make her drink whatever medicine you send, and it doesn't seem fair if it spoils the taste of her food, she hardly eats anything as it is.'

The old man chuckled. 'I can do better than that.' He got up, and began searching the shelves, humming happily to himself as he gathered ingredients from the jars and bottles into a small stone bowl. Mariana watched him curiously, her nose twitching as she caught the scents of the spices and powders he was stirring together. This magic was so different from her father's. The glassmaker breathed his magic into his creations, joining the spell and the molten glass together in the darkness of the workshop. It was an ancient tradition, and deeply valued in the city – her father was an important man. His apprentices were boys chosen for the spark of magic deep inside them. Rafa and Giorgio would spend years working with her father, mostly doing the boring, menial tasks, in the hope that their magic would one day develop the same way his had, and they would be great glassmaker-magicians themselves. There were no spells, though, not like this. Mariana's fingers shifted; she realised that she was twisting her hands together in excitement.

'You can come and watch.' Signor Nesso glanced up at her. 'You're not afraid of magic, then.'

'My father is a glassmaker-magician,' Mariana explained, hopping up and leaning over the bench to peer into the bowl. 'This looks like – like a recipe. Like our cook pounding herbs. It's so different. It's exciting,' she added shyly.

'A glassmaker. Lucky child, to be so surrounded with beautiful things.'

Mariana sniffed. 'Beautiful things that sing with magic for other people. All I'm allowed to do is dust them. Is this a spell? Do you have words for it? Or does it just happen by itself, the way my father's magic does?' She peered eagerly into the bowl. Her fingers were itching again – she wanted to stir them through the glittering powders, to feel the glow of the magic against her skin. It made her feel so happy – she could feel laughter, bubbling inside her.

'There are words, but they don't matter so much,' the old man explained, smiling down at her. Mariana wondered if he was lonely. He seemed to be enjoying the chance to show off the spell. As though he wanted someone to talk to. She glanced around the shop, suddenly realising how empty it was. She had expected a shop on the Piazza to be far busier than this.

'People don't linger in magic shops. Not usually. They sneak in, and hurry out.'

Mariana blinked, and then thought very hard about fish, to see what would happen. She didn't like the old man sifting through her thoughts.

'Yes, very nice.' He lifted his hand from the marble pestle that he'd been using to grind the ingredients together, and twisted it swiftly in the air in front of Mariana. A tiny, silvery fish appeared gasping on his palm, and Mariana squeaked.

'Well, you'd better catch the poor little thing.

Put it in a jar. There's a jug of water on the end of the bench.'

'You made him!' Mariana snatched the little fish, and dropped it into an empty glass jar, watching guiltily as it writhed about, desperate for water. She almost knocked over the jug, as she raced to fill the jar, but then she felt it lifted out of her hands, pouring a stream of water over the tiny fish. The silvery creature righted itself immediately, gliding through the glittering cascade with dreamy sweeps of its long fins.

'From your thoughts, yes. As I said before, child. I can't help it, when you're right beside me, practically yelling in my ear. But you may give the fish as a little present to your sister. I imagine your father can make her a bowl to keep him in, something more interesting than a plain old jar.'

'I'm sorry...' Mariana whispered. 'I didn't mean to be rude.'

'Nor did I.' He smiled at her as he dipped his gnarled fingers into the bowl, and stirred. 'As you suspected, I don't have many people to talk to. Most of the city hurries past my door as fast as they can.'

'Even the children?' Mariana frowned. 'Even when you make such beautiful things, like this fish, and the birds I saw fly out from under the arches before?'

'They lurk around the portico, and peer inside. Dare each other to run and stick a toe over the threshold. But very few ever come right in.'

'I would.' Mariana sighed. 'There aren't any shops like this on the island. We have pedlars who come over by boat with a few spells and amulets, and there's the glassmakers, of course, but I've never seen anyone do this sort of magic. Why are you mixing it with your hands like that?'

'Your father breathes magic into his creations; I have to touch.' He lifted his fingers out, stained purplish with the mixture. 'Pass me that little green glass bottle there.'

Mariana handed it to him, and the old man cupped his hands, whispering. Then he poured a fragrant violet liquid out from between his fingers into the bottle, stoppered it swiftly, and handed it back to Mariana.

'It smells of berries!' She stared at his hands, and then at the bowl, all perfectly clean.

'You said she wanted it to taste nice.'

'What will it do?' Mariana asked, cradling the tiny bottle between her palms.

The magician closed his hand over hers, and sighed. 'Not enough. I wish I could do more, but it will help. A little more life inside her. Less pain. Quieter sleep.'

'That's more than I hoped for,' Mariana murmured, but she could feel her eyes filling with tears. This was magic she believed in. If Signor Nessi had told her Eliza would recover, she would have trusted him – far more than any of the other travelling mages, with their outlandish claims. She trusted him now, when he said that he couldn't mend her sister. That no one could. It felt like the beginning of goodbye.

CHAPTER TWO

'LOOK AT IT... JUST LOOK at it...' Bianca Galdini turned the little bottle this way and that, so the purple liquid inside it glowed in the late afternoon sun. 'It's beautiful. And I can smell it, even with the stopper in. Flowers and fruit and – and sunlight! Like summer. Oh, this one will work, won't it, Mariana?'

Mariana swallowed to take away the dryness in her mouth. She felt so desperately sorry for her stepmother. For a moment, the deep lines between her eyes had smoothed, and there was something of the happy, singing girl that her father had married when Mariana was a five-year-old, wanting a mother. Bianca had sung to her, and danced with her, and woven ribbons in her hair. It was hard to remember all that now – she smiled so seldom, and she never danced.

'He said she'll be able to sleep peacefully, and her chest won't hurt.'

'Yes.' Her stepmother nodded impatiently. 'It'll make her well.'

Was there any point in arguing? Mariana bit her lip. She couldn't decide whether it was crueller to let her stepmother hope. Wouldn't it be better if she was ready? 'The magician said Eliza would feel better, Mama. It's not the same thing. It'll stop her hurting – but it isn't going to take away what's hurting her.'

The lines came back, even deeper, and Bianca's mouth twisted, suddenly ugly. 'No. No, that makes no sense at all. I should have gone myself, and spoken to this magician. Then he would have understood what we were asking for.'

Mariana watched as her stepmother closed her hand around the tiny green bottle, her knuckles whitening. 'Don't!' she said sharply. 'You'll break it.' She worked the bottle out from between her stepmother's clenched fingers. 'We can't waste it. It was expensive. He said it will last though – just a drop in a glass of water, every night.'

Her stepmother was staring at her, holding her fingers out in front of her, as though the bottle was still there. Then she seemed to wake up, frowning at Mariana. 'Do you know what time it is?' she snapped. 'How could it take you so long to go to one shop?'

'He had to make the spell!' Mariana protested. For once, she hadn't gone exploring, nosing around the painters' studios, watching the apprentices mix paints, and wishing she could join them. She had stayed at Signor Nesso's shop, watching him welcome back the little golden birds. They swooped through the door in a glittering stream, fluttering and twittering their way around the shelves. Mariana watched them, laughing, and fed them with the seeds the old man gave her, until at last all six of them went to roost on the curtain pole, huddling together in a sleepy mass. With a few last chirrups to Mariana and the magician, they'd tucked their heads under their wings, and then disappeared. Mariana blinked, wondering if they'd flown away again. She was sure she would have seen – and then she realised that six tiny, golden feathers were floating slowly to the floor.

'Ah, there…' the old magician murmured. 'Gather them up for me, my dear? My knees have set. This cold autumn weather. Here, put them away.' He handed her a little gold silk bag, as light and delicate as the feathers themselves.

Mariana picked up the feathers with shaking fingers. She had known that the birds were a spell – why had she been surprised, after the silver fish? But the birds were so real, so lifelike. 'You can make them real again, another day?' she whispered.

Signor Nesso bowed his head. 'Another day,' he

promised. 'The next time you come to see me, you can feed them. Dried cherries, their favourite. I will make sure I find some at the market.'

'I might not be able to buy any more spells...' Mariana mumbled. 'Once my stepmother sees that Eliza isn't getting better, she'll send me off looking for another cure, somewhere else.'

'It doesn't matter. I get by, my dear. The palace is only five minutes' walk from here, after all. Full of silly ladies-in-waiting, and foolish courtiers. All of them willing to pay a great deal of silver for love charms, and ointments to shine their hair and clear their skin. You paid me in your time. Come back and see the golden birds again, and tell me how your sister does, and if she likes her little fish.'

'She will. I expect you're right – my father will make her a beautiful fishbowl.'

Mariana smiled, remembering, and held the jar up to her stepmother. 'The magician sent this as a gift for Eliza. To amuse her, he said.'

'A gift?' Bianca stared at the tiny fish suspiciously.

'Yes. He made it out of nothing, Mama, he was so clever.'

'For me?' Eliza hauled herself up against her cushions, her breath wheezing. 'A present for me?'

'You woke her!' Mariana's stepmother hissed. 'Lie back down, dearest.'

'No! I want to see the present – show me, Mariana, what is it?'

'A little fish, look.' Mariana knelt down in front of her sister's couch, and rested the jar gently on her lap. 'See how pretty he is? The magician made him out of my thoughts – I was thinking of fish.'

'Nonsense,' snorted her stepmother.

'Why were you thinking of fish?' Eliza whispered. 'Were you hungry?' Then she shook her head anxiously as the little fish swirled in the jar. 'No one will eat you!' she assured it, putting one hand on either side of the jar and staring solemnly into the water. 'Is he hungry, Mariana? What should I feed him?'

'Just crumbs. And we ought to find him a bigger bowl to live in.'

'Papa will make one for me,' Eliza said confidently. 'A beautiful one. Could he make a bowl that shines, so I can see my little fish even when I wake up in the night? He could, I'm sure.'

'Of course he could.' Mariana glanced round at her stepmother, hoping that she would be happy to see Eliza so bright and excited – even before she had taken the medicine. But the expression on her face was horrified, and Mariana swallowed a sigh. Sometimes she wondered why her stepmother had married her father. She was terrified of the workshop – it was why she was so angry whenever she had to fetch Mariana out of it. She didn't mind the shop, since most of the glass on show wasn't obviously bespelled, but the glimmering, fantastical pieces that her father loved to create, the ones the nobility from Venice came in their boatloads to buy, those works she hated.

Probably she hadn't been given a choice, Mariana thought, as she sat by Eliza, watching the fish dive and swirl. Glassmakers were the future of the island, everyone knew that. Cosseted and protected and never allowed to leave, in case some other city learned their secrets. Signor Galdini had been a very good match. Any family would want their daughter married off to him, even if he was a widower with a little girl already.

'What's this?' Her father came out into the shop, stripping off his heavy canvas apron and handing it to Rafa.

'A pet, Papa! A magician in the city sent it to me!'

'Ah...' Mariana's father turned to her quickly, and she shook her head, one tiny movement that made his shoulders slump. He crouched down by his daughters to examine the fish, smiling and gently tapping one finger against the side of the jar. 'Poor little creature looks squashed in there. Now, where could we find him a bowl?' He made a puzzled face at Eliza, and she pounded his arm with one weak little fist.

'Make one, Papa, please! A bowl that shines like a lamp!'

'Ah...' He stood up, nodding. 'Mariana, you take the jar, while I carry the signorina here. Rafa, open the door. Tell Giorgio not to let the fire die down. One last piece.' He scooped up Eliza in a nest of blankets, and carried her out across the little courtyard to the workshop. Mariana hurried behind him with the fish in the jar, with her stepmother murmuring anxiously after them.

Papa nestled Eliza into the glassblower's chair, an ancient wooden one with long arms to rest the pontil rods on. She curled up there, looking around eagerly – she came into the workshop even less often than Mariana. 'Will you make me a fishbowl?' she asked hopefully. 'I can watch?'

'The heat in here – it's not good for her.' Bianca fussed around her little daughter, patting her forehead anxiously, and fiddling with the blankets.

Eliza pulled away. 'Mama, stop! I want to see the fire!'

'Oh, ssshhh,' Papa scoffed. 'It won't do her any harm for a few minutes. She'll like to see us make her toy. Don't fuss over her.'

'I'll fetch her some water, Mama, and put the medicine in it. That will cool her down,' Mariana suggested, and hurried back across the courtyard to bring the bottle and pour water from the jug in the kitchen. She pulled the stopper out of the bottle, smiling as a waft of perfume spiralled up to meet her, and dripped one drop into the glass of water. It sank slowly to the bottom, trailing wisps of lilac, and gradually the whole glassful turned a rich, deep violet. Mariana walked back to the workshop, cupping the precious glass between her hands.

Her father and the two apprentices were fussing lovingly around the furnace, stoking it up to melt the glass ready for shaping. The great beehive dome-shape crackled and buzzed with the heat of the fire inside, and her father peered through the little sliding door at the molten glass in the crucible, hissing through his teeth.

'Ready.' He held out his hand, and Rafa was there at once with a blowpipe for him to gather up the molten glass. Eliza clapped her hands excitedly as her father drew out a yellow-white ball of glass, soft and glowing like honey in the sun.

Standing behind Eliza and her stepmother, Mariana found herself reaching out towards the ball of glass, as she had yearned for the magic in the very walls of Signor Nesso's shop. It shone even more brightly than the little golden birds, radiant with heat and powerful magic. She wanted it so. She could feel it calling to her, and something in her heart called back. Why couldn't her father see that there was magic in her too? Couldn't she make something just as beautiful as this?

Then Eliza turned back, pulling at Mariana's skirt with her thin fingers. 'Look, Mariana, it's burning! The glass is on fire!'

Mariana shook herself, feeling dazed. What had happened? Was that what magic felt like?

'Mariana!'

The strangeness faded, and Mariana smiled at her little sister. 'No, it's just hot. It's so hot it looks as if it's burning, that's all. That glass will be the fishbowl, when Papa's shaped it.'

'Your bowl!' Eliza whispered to the little fish, and Mariana could have sworn that he pressed himself closer to the side of the jar to watch.

Her father shaped the ball of glass in a cup of soaked wood, then worked it on the marble block, rolling it round and round to smooth and cool the sides. Then he dipped it into a bowl of yellow glass chips – 'To look like the seashore, Eliza,' he murmured, as he plunged the pipe back into the glory-hole on the other side of the furnace to melt the glass again.

This time when he drew it out, he blew down the pipe, stretching out the ball of glass into a bubble. Mariana was never sure whether this was magic, or just pure skill, but it seemed like magic to her. The bubble grew, and Eliza squeaked with delight as Giorgio laid out green glass rods, and fantastical glass flowers for her father to roll on to the glass. 'Seaweed and anemones,' Mariana whispered to her admiringly.

'Your fish will have a little palace to live in. I'll fetch him some real seaweed too.'

The great glass bubble swelled, coated with streaks and whorls of colour, until at last her father nodded to Rafa. The apprentice dipped a metal rod in the crucible of molten glass, and stuck it gently to the base of the bowl, so that her father could break it off the blowpipe. They heated it over and over, pulling and shaping the mouth of the bowl into a delicately curled lip, the pictures on the outside stretching and growing each time, until at last their father carried the great bowl to Eliza. 'Not to touch yet, little one. It needs to cool in the annealing oven, or it'll crack when we pour in the water for your fish. But tomorrow night it will be ready, I promise. And you shall have glittering pebbles of glass, and Rafa and Giorgio will make you crystal trees for your fish to swim around.'

'I wish Signor Nesso could see it,' Mariana murmured. 'You should make more of these, Papa, for the court ladies to keep fish in. It's the most beautiful bowl I've ever seen. Oh, Eliza, look – the seaweed moves!'

Her father chuckled wearily as he carried the bowl away to cool in the annealing oven on the far side of the furnace, the furthest from the fire. Mariana watched the bowl in his hands, the fronds of weed shifting in the imaginary currents of the glass. She didn't envy Eliza, though her father had never made her something so beautiful. Even Rafa and Giorgio would do anything for her little sister now.

Eliza had gone to sleep, with the jar standing close on the chest beside her bed. There was a little colour in her cheeks, but Mariana wasn't sure if it was from excitement or the medicine Signor Nesso had made.

Mariana left her stepmother watching over Eliza, and padded down the stairs and out through the yard on to the quay. She was finding it harder and harder to spend time with her sister, even though she could see they had so little time left. Seeing Eliza weaken every day hurt. Every time her sister ran out of breath before she could finish a sentence, something tugged at Mariana's heart. Sometimes it was just easier not to look. Shrugging her cloak around her shoulders, Mariana hurried down the stone-built part of the quay, making for the wilder edges. Murano wasn't one island, but a clutch of tiny islets, joined together with bridges. As the fame of the island's glassmaker-mages grew, more and more of the land was being bought up and built on, but there were wild, empty stretches too. Out here the sea lapped against long stretches of muddy sand, instead of fine paved quays fringed with boats. It was almost dark, and she could see the lights of Venice shining across the water.

She sat down on the sand, spreading out her cloak to protect her dress a little, and hunched up, with her arms around her knees, staring out at those glowing lights. Signor Nesso was over there, somewhere. Murano was on the other side of the city to Piazza San Marco, so none of those lights would be his, but still. If she half-closed her eyes, she could make the lamplight look like golden birds, swooping out into the darkness.

'He'd let me do magic,' she whispered to herself. 'He didn't mind that I wasn't a boy. He said he liked talking to me.'

Sighing, she picked up a piece of driftwood, and started to scratch patterns in the sand – swirling shapes today, like the waterweeds her father had magicked on to the glass. She could feel a tiny burning bubble inside her, as she remembered the patterns on the molten glass, and a smile curved her lips. It was coming back – it was real! She hadn't imagined the echo of the magic inside her. But then she threw the stick down in the sand.

She would be just as good an apprentice as Rafa and Giorgio, she was sure. She knew all the equipment in the workshop, even though she was hardly ever allowed in there. She had watched her father crafting the bowl that afternoon, and found the glowing yellow-white of the molten glass burning inside her, pulsing with her own heartbeat. She wanted it. She wanted magic like her father's. She wanted to learn, like Rafa and Giorgio. To make glass, or to carve wood, to paint – to make *something*. What if that white-hot seed in her heart died down, the way glass did? It cooled and set – and often, *often*, if there was a fault in the glass, it shattered.

That might happen to her. If she had to keep on dusting the shop over and over, perhaps being allowed into the workshop to carry a message to her father every day or so, the strange glow inside her would crystallise, and break into tiny, piercing shards.

'I *could* do magic too. Why can't a girl be a glassmaker?'

She had asked her father so many times over the years, but he always brushed the question aside with a laugh. It wasn't even worth considering. Glassmaking was a man's work, everyone knew. Women got married. Mariana would marry the son of another glassmaker, to keep the strain of magic in the family. And her father would go on praying for a son.

'I could go to the duchess,' Mariana whispered. 'She'd understand. She has the most powerful magic in Venice. She could make a decree, she could tell everyone.' But deep inside, Mariana was almost sure that even a decree from Duchess Olivia wouldn't make her father and his cronies listen. There would be some sort of protest – they'd argue that girls couldn't take the heat of the furnaces, or perhaps that carrying about the heavy glassware might weaken them for childbearing. The glassmakers of Murano were too valuable to offend.

Mariana sniffed miserably, and felt a tear slide down the side of her nose. She reached up to brush it away, and then stared at her hand.

The tear was glass. A tiny, perfect, crystal glass tear drop.

With shaking fingers, she picked it up, and rested it in her palm, watching it roll to and fro. It glittered in the faint lights of the houses far behind her, glowing with its own blue-white fire, brighter than her father's furnace.

Mariana clicked open the silver locket she wore around her neck, studded with jewel-like *millefiori* glass, and slid the teardrop inside. It was a sign, she was sure of it. A promise – to herself. Whatever her father said, it *proved* there was magic inside her.

And there were other places to make magic than Murano.

CHAPTER THREE

'MARIANA, WIPE THAT DIRT OFF your face. Run to the kitchen and tell Lena we need honey cakes, and wine.'

'Who's coming?' Mariana peered around her stepmother, trying to see out of the open shutters. She was practically sure that her face was clean, Mama was just fussing.

'Hurry!' But then Bianca relented. 'Count Renigo, and his wife, *and* their spoiled little daughter – one of their footmen came ahead to warn us. I'll need you to watch that girl, Mariana, last time they were here she broke a platter she was fiddling with, and of course they didn't pay.'

Mariana made a face. She remembered. Mama had been furious, though she hadn't shown it to their rich customers. She had simply called Mariana and the maid to sweep up the mess, while she hurried the count and countess on to look at something even more expensive. 'I'll try. But she's not used to anyone ever telling her no – how do I stop her if she wants to pick things up?'

'Oh, I don't know – just try!' Her stepmother hurried about, rearranging the pieces on display, and whipping off her streaked apron. The medicine had helped Eliza to sleep well the night before, but this morning she was pale and quiet and didn't want to get up. Bianca clearly ached to be upstairs looking after her.

Mariana sighed, and went to give the cook the message. By the time she slipped back into the shop, the noble family were at the door, and Bianca was curtseying, murmuring how honoured they were that Count Renigo had deigned to return to their humble establishment – all the while peering sideways at Julia, the count's careless daughter. Mariana managed not to smirk as she dropped her curtsey too.

Julia didn't look as though she was going to be a problem this time – she stood in the middle of the shop, her shoulders hunched, scowling. The very picture of a child who had been dragged out on an errand by her parents, and was going to make it quite clear that she didn't want to be there.

'Would you like a honey cake, my lady?' Mariana asked her, seeing that Lena had left a tray on the table at the back of the shop.

'No,' the child growled, kicking at the floorboards with her jewelled slipper. Then she seemed to feel guilty – or perhaps she thought her mother might have heard her. 'I'm not hungry, thank you.'

It seemed that the count and countess had come to make a special order, for wine glasses, all to be perfectly matched, and of the finest workmanship.

Countess Renigo was browsing through the shelves, exclaiming at the different shapes and patterns. Mariana's stepmother flinched every time she touched anything – she was clearly in a particularly anxious mood.

The countess picked up a delicate goblet, the bowl patterned in net-like *reticello*, and held it out to her husband. 'Here, my dear, look! See, the stem is a dolphin – what if Signor Galdini could make them as cats?'

'Our coat of arms has cats on it,' Julia muttered gloomily to Mariana. 'The house is covered in them. Except I'm not allowed to have a real one because they make Mama sneeze. Father keeps his three cats shut up in his study, but they're always sneaking out and going to lie on her bed. That's why her nose is so pink.'

'What on earth did she marry your father for, then?' Mariana answered without thinking. She had been watching the careless way the countess was twirling the goblet, and hoping there would be no more breakages. Then she realised what she'd said, and to whom, gasped, and folded her lips tightly together. But Julia didn't seem to mind. She eyed Mariana curiously, as though someone who said what they thought was a refreshing change.

'I think she probably thought that for that much money she could put up with anything.' Julia smirked, enjoying Mariana's shocked look.

'My lady! You shouldn't say that sort of thing!' Mariana hissed. 'It's very disrespectful. Though I do know what you mean.' She eyed Julia sideways, trying to work out how old she was. Perhaps seven or eight – but she sounded older.

'Disrespectful but true. My mama's family are noble but very, very poor. And don't worry, she's not listening. They don't listen to me.'

'Julia!' The countess turned round. 'Oh, there you are.' Both girls assumed identical pious expressions, as though they had been discussing embroidery, or something equally innocent.

'Are you nearly finished, Mama?' Julia asked, her

voice well on the way to a whine.

'We'll be a little while, my sweet.' The countess looked at her daughter anxiously, and then glanced around at the shelves, as if she'd only just realised that they'd brought her into a shop full of fragile and expensive glass.

'Would you like my daughter to take the young lady for a walk while you consider, my lady?' Bianca suggested, ignoring Mariana's horror-struck expression. What if she ran off? Or fell in the canal? Mariana knew exactly who would get the blame.

'Oh… Yes, I suppose…' Countess Renigo looked properly at Mariana for the first time, and appeared to approve of what she saw. 'Yes. That would be most helpful.' She turned to Julia, whispering instructions to the younger girl as she fussed with her mantle and velvet cap.

'Where am I supposed to take her?' Mariana hissed in her stepmother's ear.

'I don't know! Out of here! The church. Go and show her the mosaics.'

'Oh, very well.' Mariana curtseyed again to the countess, and opened the door for Julia.

'I won't fall in the canal.'

'How did you know I...' Mariana stared at her, wondering if she had the same mindreading magic as Signor Nesso.

'I could see the way you were looking at it, and then at me. Where are we going?'

'The church. It's across the bridge on the other side of the canal, the church of Santa Maria and San Donato.'

'A church?' Julia moaned. 'Must we?'

'It's pretty,' Mariana said, feeling a little affronted, as she led Julia on to the bridge. 'It's old, and there are mosaics.'

'All churches have mosaics. I've seen them.'

'Well, this one has dragon bones, so there,' Mariana snapped back. 'Don't tell me you've seen those in any other church in Venice.'

'*Dragon* bones?' the smaller girl scoffed. 'You're making it up. There isn't any such thing.'

'Of course there is! What was the Leviathan that Duchess Olivia and Lady Mia banished out of the city five years ago, if he wasn't a water dragon?'

Julia sniffed dismissively. 'He didn't have any wings.'

'This one did. He wasn't as big as the Leviathan, but he was fearsome, and poisonous. He was poisoning a well, on an island. Not this one, somewhere else.' Mariana couldn't remember exactly where. 'The saint got rid of him…' She stared at Julia, drawing herself up impressively. 'By spitting in his eye! He was so holy that the dragon just keeled over and died.'

Julia looked as though she wanted to argue again, but wasn't quite sure where to start.

'And his bones are in this church,' Mariana went on quickly. 'The dragon's bones too. Some of them.'

'Show me,' Julia demanded. 'I think you're just making it up.'

'Ssshhh,' Mariana told her impressively. 'Don't talk in here. The priest will tell you off.'

'He wouldn't dare,' Julia muttered, but she did hush as they hurried round the curved apse at the back of the church, and through the main doors. 'The mosaic is pretty,' she admitted, shifting her skirts to look at the patchwork of precious marble inlaid across the floor.

'Look up, then.' Mariana pointed to the arched apse, where Santa Maria was staring down at them, surrounded by gold tiles.

Julia shrugged. 'All churches have the Virgin Mary,' she pointed out. 'The patterns all over the floor are more interesting. And where are those bones you promised me?'

'Down there below the Holy Mother. Behind the altar.' She beckoned Julia up the aisle. 'Here, look. Hanging from the bottom of that picture.'

Julia peered at them around the enormous stone altar, where the saint's bones rested. 'I thought it would be a whole skeleton,' she said, gazing disappointed at the three great ribs. 'Though they are quite big, I suppose.'

'They're huge!' Mariana glared at her. She was beginning to see now that Julia wouldn't be happy with anything less than a whole, live dragon flying round and round her head. 'I'd better take you back. Your mother must have finished looking at wine glasses by now.'

'I doubt it.' But Julia shrugged. 'Take me back if you like. I don't mind.'

Mariana eyed the younger girl sideways as they tiptoed out of the church. She had a feeling that she did mind – there was something hard, almost brittle, about the tone of her voice. But for the life of her, she couldn't see why. 'Shouldn't you have a maid?' she asked suddenly. 'I thought all the nobility had servants waiting around to pick up a handkerchief if they dropped it. You should have a lady's maid. Or a nurse, I suppose.'

'I'm eight! That's far too old for a nursemaid!'

'A governess, then – something.'

'My maid has given up and gone home to her mother,' Julia muttered. 'So until my mama finds

another one, she is dragging me around everywhere.'
Her voice went whispery-sweet, like her mother's.
'And it's all my own fault. If only I was better behaved,
and not such a nasty-tempered little thing, my maids
wouldn't keep leaving, would they?'

'Oh.' Mariana blinked. 'Are you that bad?' she
added at last.

Julia grinned at her, and suddenly raced away over
the bridge. 'Worse!'

'Don't you dare fall in the canal!' Mariana shrieked,
dashing after her.

'Who was that girl you were playing with?' Eliza
asked, pouting a little as she stared up at Mariana.

Mariana smiled at her, and stroked Eliza's damp
hair away from her hot little face. 'How did you know
I was playing with her?'

'I heard you – the window was open. I tried to get
up and see, but I was too tired.'

Mariana nodded. 'You mustn't get up. You know
what Mama said.'

'Until I'm better,' Eliza agreed wearily. 'It's taking a long time.'

'Yes.' Mariana tried not to let her voice wobble. 'I know it doesn't seem fair, being stuck in bed.'

'So who was she?'

'*That* was Lady Julia, the daughter of Count and Countess Renigo. Mama sent me to look after her. Do you remember, a few months back, when Mama was in such a temper because a little girl broke a platter in the shop?'

Eliza rolled her eyes. 'She was fuming. It was that girl, then?'

'Yes. Mama sent me to look after her and take her out of the shop, in case she did it again.' Mariana laughed. 'Apparently, she's so naughty that her maid has given up her post in disgust, and so the countess has to look after her dreadful daughter all by herself.' She sighed, and stroked Eliza's hand. 'I would much rather have been playing with you, I promise. She kept teasing me, standing on the very edge of the quay and pretending she was going to overbalance into the canal. And then of course she did overbalance and I had to haul her back again before she went in. I'm exhausted.'

'Lie down here next to me,' Eliza suggested, patting her pillow, and Mariana curled up beside her. She could feel the fever burning up inside Eliza even through her coverlet. The violet medicine didn't seem to be helping as much as it had when Eliza first took it, the week before. It wasn't keeping her temperature down, and although she wasn't complaining of any pain, she was spending more and more time asleep. She seemed to be slowly curling herself inwards. Mariana could feel her drawing away.

'Do you think she would have liked me?' Eliza whispered, her voice a pale thread.

'Yes. Of course she would. But she'd have been jealous of your pretty, curly hair.' Mariana swallowed. Eliza's hair trailed across the pillow now, lank and straw-like. Mariana wound it around her finger, trying to remember the gleaming softness of the curls.

Surely Eliza's hair had still been smooth and glossy a week or so ago. Things seemed to be changing so fast.

'Where's my fish?' Eliza whispered. If her sister hadn't been asking the same question for the last day and a half, Mariana wouldn't have understood the wheezing little breath.

'He's just here. Shall I help you touch his bowl?'

'Mmm.'

Mariana lifted her sister's hot little hand, and placed it against the glass. The silvery fish swam across the bowl, nudging at her fingers through the patterned glass, and Eliza's mouth curled in a tiny smile. Then she slumped back on her pillows again, and Mariana cast a desperate glance back at her father and stepmother.

Her father stepped up next to the bed, and put his arm around Mariana's shoulders. 'It won't be long,' he murmured.

'Couldn't we give her some more of the medicine?' Mariana pleaded, looking round at her stepmother as well. But she was standing at the end of the bed, clutching the wooden bed-frame, staring at Eliza with blank eyes. Mariana could hear her whispering, 'No, no, no…'

'We have to be ready,' Mariana's father said, reaching out his hand to her, but she ignored him, and he hung his head. 'Mariana, watch your sister for a moment. And your mother. I have to go to the workshop. I'll be a minute or two, no more.'

'The workshop?' Mariana stared at him. He was thinking of work, now? 'Father, please…'

'You'll see. Just watch them.' He hurried out of the room, and she heard his footsteps thundering downstairs. Mariana bit her lip, looking at her stepmother. Her face was so white and set, it was frightening. Mariana had to force herself to lean over and touch her fingers. 'Mama. Please. Come and sit with her. Hold her hand.'

But her stepmother flinched, as though Mariana's touch burned her, and didn't move. She just kept up that fixed, dreadful stare at Eliza. It was a relief when her father hurried back in, cradling a glowing bubble of molten glass in his bare hands.

'What is that?' Mariana whispered. 'It'll burn you, put it down!' Her father's arms were mottled with scars, old and faded now, but still angry-looking. The molten glass should be sticking to his skin, but there was no hissing sound, no smell of burning. It could have been an apple, or a stone from the yard.

'It won't burn,' he muttered grimly. 'It's a spell, Mariana. Not one I can do too often. But I need it. I can't bear to let her go, not for ever. Not completely.'

'What are you going to— Eliza!' Mariana suddenly gasped. Her sister's eyes had opened, a soft blue still, but now strangely clouded. She seemed to be trying to focus – as though she was looking for someone.

'Mama!' Mariana hissed, and gave up trying to coax her stepmother. Instead she grabbed her wrist, yanking her grip away from the foot of the bed, and pushing her towards Eliza. They had spent so long tiptoeing around Eliza, lifting her gently, whispering so as not to wake her. It didn't matter any more. What mattered was that Eliza saw her mama was there.

Eliza smiled again, and then the awareness faded out of her eyes, leaving them lifeless, emptier than the shards of broken blue glass in the spoils bin downstairs.

Mariana's father leaned over, and held the bubble of molten glass close to Eliza's mouth, in time to catch her last faint sighing breath. His tears splashed down on to the burning glass and sizzled, and that strange little sound seemed to jolt his wife out of her silence. She looked down at Eliza, lifeless on her pillows, and screamed and screamed.

CHAPTER FOUR

MARIANA SAT CURLED UP IN the corner of the workshop, listening to her father as he muttered instructions to the boys. She should be working in the shop, or sewing, or doing something. But she couldn't bring herself to move. And no one would come to tell her off, to hustle her out. Her stepmother was sitting on Eliza's little couch at the back of the shop – staring blindly at the shelves. She probably hadn't even noticed that Mariana wasn't there.

Mariana's father had found a clean shirt for Rafa and sent him to deal with the customers, and for once Rafa hadn't complained. Eliza's death had cast a quiet sadness over the whole house – even the glass Mariana's father was working with seemed to have changed colour; it glowed blue-white coming out of the furnace now, cold and cheerless. Mariana wasn't sure if the pieces her father was making would ever find customers – they were beautiful, but there was no warmth in them, no life.

The glass bubble that had captured Eliza's last breath was hanging from a hook on one of the ceiling beams, spinning lightly in the air currents from the furnace. It had cooled to a clear, pale lilac – as though Eliza's breath had been sweetened by the medicine she'd taken. It looked like one of the glass floats that the fishermen used to mark their nets – except that there was a faint frosty swirling under the glass. It shifted and coiled, and Mariana couldn't stop watching it. In the week since Eliza's death, she had spent almost all of her time in that one dusty corner, her eyes fixed on the bubble. It seemed to change with the light – sometimes she was sure that the breath under the glass was fighting to be free, the way it spun and beat against the sides. Other times the sun shone clearly though the purple glass, and the air inside shifted serenely to and fro.

Was there any part of Eliza inside that glass? Mariana didn't know – she didn't even know what she wanted the answer to be. Of course she wished that there was something of Eliza still there with them, but her little sister had been so tired and fragile. Wasn't it better to let her go?

'Mariana.'

She jumped, gasping as she looked up to see her father standing over her.

'Sweetheart, you've been curled in the corner all morning. Go on out to the kitchens. Ask Lena for a bit of cake – some for me and Giorgio too. I've no doubt Rafa will already have begged as much as he can eat.'

'I'll fetch some for you.' Mariana hauled her herself

up, wincing as the blood rushed back into her numb feet. 'But everything seems to make me think of Eliza. How she'd beg for cake, and then leave half the slice, all crumbled up. And then I'd moan at her for not just giving it to me.'

Her father chuckled. 'She ate like a little bird,' he agreed sadly. 'We should have known – we did know. I thought I'd be ready, when she left us, but perhaps we never could be.' His face shifted, and he sighed. 'How is your mama? I should go and talk to her…'

'I don't think she can hear us,' Mariana murmured. 'She's somewhere else. Papa, do you think part of her can have gone with Eliza? Is that possible?'

'Who knows… I shall have to do something.' He pressed his hands to his temples, as if his head ached. 'She won't even let me hold her. I don't know how to help. You're right, I think. She spent all her time fretting and worrying about Eliza, and now that's all been torn away from her. Why didn't I try to talk to her before, Mariana? She must have known…'

'She always believed something would make Eliza

better,' Mariana whispered. 'She couldn't let herself see what was happening.'

Her father nodded, and then smiled a little as a streak of sunlight caught the bubble of violet glass. 'Little one,' he murmured fondly. Then his gaze sharpened, and he glanced over at the furnace, where Giorgio was stoking the fire.

'What is it? You're not going to melt it down?' Mariana asked sharply.

'No, no, of course not. I was just thinking… Perhaps there is something I can do to help your mama. She needs something to love.'

'She doesn't like dogs, Papa, and a cat would jump about in the shop,' Mariana pointed out, thinking of Count Renigo's escaping cats. 'I put Eliza's fish bowl on a stand by the couch, but I don't think it's helping. Should I go back to Signor Nesso?' she asked. 'I could ask him to make something for grief. Not just for Mama,' she added sadly. 'For all of us.'

'Mmm.' Her father frowned. 'From what you said of him before, the old magician has too much sense.

He might well say we should be grieving. Would you want to take a potion and forget Eliza?'

'No, I didn't mean that.' Mariana frowned at him. 'You know I didn't. I just don't want to feel the way I do. There's a hole in me – and it's worse for Mama. Eliza was everything to her.' She blinked to herself for a moment, realising that this was true. Her father and stepmother were polite to each other, they never fought, hardly said a cross word. But they never laughed together either. Lena's admirer, one of the boys from the bakery, was always turning up to leave a flower for her, or a loaf of fancy bread, or just to whisper in her ear so that she giggled and dropped things. Her parents were never like that. Papa spent most of his time in the workshop, and Mama had lived to fuss over Eliza. Mariana had always assumed that was how all families behaved, but surely there ought to be something more?

She looked up uncomfortably at her father, wondering if she'd upset him, but he didn't seem to have noticed. He was staring at the bubble of glass, and whistling through his teeth. At last he pulled out his knife and cut down the glass, cradling it in one huge hand, still whistling.

'What are you going to do?' Mariana asked urgently. She was almost tempted to snatch it away from him. The air inside the bubble was swirling faster and faster, as if it could feel her anxiety.

'You hold it,' her father murmured, pressing it into her hands. 'Look after it for me a moment. Giorgio! Where's he gone? I need you, boy, stop slacking and get over here.'

Giorgio appeared from out in the yard, looking shifty with cake crumbs around his mouth. 'What?' he muttered. 'I was only gone a minute. I'm starving.'

'Get Rafa – I don't care about the shop. Lena can serve any customers, I need both of you. Mariana, stay back out of the way, my treasure.'

Mariana stepped back obediently, her cheeks reddening a little at the endearment. Her father hardly ever called her pretty names. Why was he so bright and alive again all of a sudden? She cuddled the violet glass close against her dress, her heart thumping. Her father and the apprentices were fussing around the furnace, laying out the tools ready and checking the temperature of the melting glass. There was an excitement in the air that she had not felt since Eliza's death. This piece would be different. Her father drew out a fat globe of glass, twirling it lovingly, and began to roll it on the marble slab, flattening the side to a cylinder, while the boys watched, mouths pursed, ready to hand him the tweezers and shears. Mariana couldn't tell what the piece was supposed to be; it looked a strange sort of lump, studded with holes, but her father seemed happy. He left Rafa murmuring to it, cupping his hands above the glass and sweet-talking it to keep it warm. They were going to add more pieces, then. Mariana peered curiously at the next ball of glass to come out – smaller this time, and smoothed out to a slimmer cylinder. Then her father snatched the tweezers from Giorgio, and began to shape the end of the piece, pulling out strands of molten glass while Mariana edged a little forward, trying to see what they were making. A starfish? Like the one Rafa had proudly presented to Eliza for her fishbowl? Mariana swallowed, remembering the way Eliza had laughed and clapped at his cleverness.

Hands. It was a hand. On the end of a chubby little pink-brown glass arm. There were even nails – she caught her breath, watching as they tipped each tiny finger with a droplet of paler glass.

She could see now that the first piece was a body – they were making a doll. She had one of her own, that her father had made for her years before, but much smaller and simpler than this. Mariana stretched out her own arm, measuring. The doll would be almost child-size. Just a little smaller than Eliza.

She chewed her lip, watching as they formed another perfect little arm, the fingers half closed this time, so that the doll could hold something in her hand. Perhaps a flower. Her father moved the tweezers like a paintbrush, incising perfect creases on the backs of the glass baby's fingers – it was the finest workmanship Mariana had ever seen. She crept impatiently closer as they shaped legs, and tiny feet that reminded her of the baby angels in the church paintings. The face – she wanted to see the face, Eliza's face. She was sure that was what her father was making. A little glass girl for her stepmother to love.

Her father staggered a little as he pulled out the last ball of glass, his hands shaking as he lifted it from the furnace, so that Giorgio leaped to hold his arm, and Rafa faltered a moment in the whispering. Mariana caught a glimpse of her father's face, realising for the first time how much magic he was pouring into this. He was pale, his forehead shining with sweat, but he turned the glass expertly in the wooden cup that Giorgio was holding ready, shaping the ball into a smooth oval. They seemed to heat the glass over and over, plunging it back into the furnace after every careful pass with the tweezers. She couldn't see – and she didn't dare go closer, in case she got in the way.

Giorgio clipped two slices from a white glass rod, laying them on the marble for her father to pick up with the glass, and Mariana pressed the bubble of Eliza's breath closer to her heart. The rod was striped inside, white, blue, black, so each slice was one of Eliza's soft grey-blue eyes. When Mariana and her stepmother had taken the baby out to show off, all the mothers had envied Eliza's pretty eyes and soft brown curls, her neat little nose.

Mariana's father turned the glass face towards her as he carried it back to the furnace, and she stepped back in sudden fright. That was Eliza. A tiny, delicate, perfect Eliza gazing back at her. Mariana realised that she was murmuring to herself, a frightened squeaky sound as she cradled the glass ball against her chest. A wordless prayer, and she didn't even know what for.

'The hair,' her father wheezed hoarsely. 'Brown glass, we'll tease it out into curls.'

Giorgio nodded, putting a tiny crucible of brown

glass in the furnace to melt. Mariana's father slumped into the glassblower's chair, wiping his forehead with the tail of his shirt.

'We'll need you in a moment,' he said, nodding to Mariana, and her heart jumped inside her. The strange fear faded a little. It was only a doll, after all…

'I can help?'

'I need you to break that – when I tell you.' He gestured to the bubble of violet glass, and Mariana slumped with disappointment. That was all. He didn't mean for her to take any part in the making.

'It's ready, I think.' Giorgio beckoned to her father to look at the melting glass, and he heaved himself wearily out of the chair.

'Yes. This is the last part – Mariana, be ready.'

Mariana looked down at the purple glass in her hands. In her disappointment, she hadn't listened properly to what her father meant. They were breaking the bubble? *She* had to break it? She clutched it tightly as she watched Giorgio add knots of brown glass to the glass girl's head, so that her father could shape them into curls. The tweezers drew them out like pouring syrup, and Mariana smiled in spite of herself. Eliza's hair had shone just like that in the sun, and hers did too – it was one of the few things that made them look like sisters.

'Now, Rafa. All the pieces together,' her father called urgently. Mariana sucked her bottom lip under her teeth – she could see her father's strength was failing now.

Slowly, hissing to himself with the effort, Rafa moved the glass pieces into position, lining up the legs and arms. The doll lay there, headless and sad, but still shimmering with magic. She looked as though she could stand up, any moment. She was a she – almost a person already. Mariana shuddered. For a panicked second, she considered flinging the bubble of glass on to the floor.

But her father was beckoning to her already. Giorgio was about to knock the glass head off the blowpipe – then all the pieces would be together.

Mariana moved towards them, her feet moving

without her meaning them to, as though she was sleepwalking. She was caught up in the power of the magic. The glass girl had to be finished. The pieces wanted to be together – and the breath in the bubble was pouring itself from side to side, beating against its glass prison, eager to join the spell.

Her father stroked his hands over the joins in the glass limbs, the soft ridges of the glass collarbone, where the child's head met her shoulders. The glass softened and knitted together, the joins invisible. Magic was gleaming all over his skin and his creation's, tiny glittering sparks floating out into the dimness of the workshop. The child glowed.

'Now!' Mariana's father reached out to her, catching her sleeve. 'Crack it against the marble. Like an egg. Now, Mariana!'

Mariana did as he asked. She still wasn't sure – she couldn't help thinking of Signor Nesso, and his warnings about dark magic, magic that tried to play with life and death – but her father's face was anguished. She couldn't disappoint him. And this could be her only chance to mend Mama.

She struck the glass bubble sharply against the edge of the marble slab, and a faint pattern of cracks spidered over the purple glass, frosting it with silver.

'Now that it's open, press it into her chest. The glass is soft, it won't break,' her father assured her as she hesitated. 'Now!'

The glass child lay shimmering on the marble, pale and still. Looking at her close up, a little baby glass sister, Mariana's doubts faded away. She was so like Eliza – but her eyes were flat, as Eliza's had been in that last moment. She needed the breath, it wasn't in Mariana's heart to deny her. She pushed the glass bubble against the pink-gold glass flesh, flinching a little. She almost expected blood – or some strange glass ichor. But the purple glass melted gently through the child's skin, and disappeared.

All at once, a creamy violet glow ran through her, darkening her cheeks, the palms of her delicate hands, the soles of her tiny feet. Her fingers twitched – and she sat up.

Mariana's stepmother had kept all Eliza's clothes, laid away lovingly in a wooden chest, scented with sachets of sweet herbs. Mariana looked in at her on her way upstairs, peering around the door into the shop. She was lying on the little couch, her head resting against the cushions, just as Eliza's had always been. Mariana had pressed her face against those cushions several times over the last week too. She could just catch the scent of the lavender infusion that her stepmother had always used to wash Eliza's hair. She clenched her nails into her palms. This had to work – how could it not work? The little glass girl was Eliza come to life – but even more perfect. How could Eliza's mother not love her?

Mariana ran up the stairs to Eliza's bedroom. She had spent the whole week not even looking at the door of the tiny room, but now she had to. She stepped in reluctantly, looking around. The sheets and coverlet were gone from the bed – now it was just a bare wooden frame, with a wool-stuffed mattress rolled up on top of it. It was horribly bare.

Mariana pulled the wooden box out from under the bed, easing up the hinged lid and smiling as she saw the dresses laid on the top. These were the clothes Eliza had been wearing last year – she had grown, just a little, and these had been too small for her. The glass Eliza was smaller, so they should fit. Mariana pulled out a little petticoat with a trimming of cotton lace, and a frock, a little faded but still good. Cream linen with a faint lilac stripe – the perfect colour.

When she got back to the workshop, her father and the two boys were still staring at their creation. They looked confused, almost amazed at what they'd made. The doll – girl – Eliza? – Mariana didn't know what to call her – was huddled on the marble slab, her arms wrapped around her knees. She looked round as she heard Mariana running in, and she looked frightened.

Mariana stopped. She was a doll. She couldn't be frightened. But her eyes were wide, and the pretty flush had faded out of her cheeks, and her mouth was set in an odd tight line. Exactly the way Eliza's did when she was unhappy, when one of the others had teased her because she couldn't run.

'Oh, don't look like that!' Mariana forgot to be frightened of her. She dropped the clothes on the marble slab, and caught the strange little creature up in her arms. 'You're lovely, you're our own. We won't let anyone hurt you.'

She was strange to hold – like Eliza and like Mariana's old glass doll, but somehow not the same as either of them. The glass girl was solid. Her skin didn't have the softness of Eliza's, there was no give to her. But she didn't seem fragile, like Mariana's doll Mikki. She had broken so often that she was all glass patches, and Papa had said she'd better live on the top of the wardrobe, out of harm's way. Mariana hadn't minded – she had grown out of carrying Mikki around anyway. The glass girl nestled into Mariana's neck, snuggling against her like a kitten. Her glass curls rang against each other like little bells.

Mariana smiled, and then caught Giorgio and

Rafa whispering to each other. 'What?' She glared at them. 'Don't look at her like that.'

The little glass child turned her head, to see where Mariana was looking. 'What are they doing?' she whispered in Mariana's ear, in a high, musical voice. It was not like Eliza's voice at all, and it sounded strange coming from Eliza's pursed, plump, little mouth.

'You talk?' Mariana stared down at her, shocked.

'She's a marvel,' Rafa said, with a whistle. 'Sir, you've never made anything like this before, never. She's a magical creature. Like that cat the duchess made. She's a Grand Working, she is. You'll have to report her to the Duchess's Council.'

'Report her?' Mariana turned the little girl away, shielding her from Rafa, as though he might snatch her. 'What do you mean? There's nothing wrong – why should we have to report her?' She looked down into Eliza's eyes, glittering in glass, and tried to put out of her mind the strangeness, the eerie panic that had seized her when she first realised what her father was doing. What harm could there be? She was just a doll.

A doll that talked, and probably walked. And thought, and felt, and made people love her...

'Rafa's right,' her father muttered. 'I didn't think this through. I wanted to help my Bianca, that was all. I wanted a memory of Eliza. I must have been mad. Who knows what we've done? I'll have half the city down here, priests and scholars and councilmen. I only missed little Eliza...' He pressed his hands against his forehead again, and groaned. Then he slumped down in the glassmaker's chair.

'Why are they angry?' the bell-like voice whispered again. Higher. Frightened.

'Because you're strange,' Mariana murmured back. 'Strange and special. Do you understand what happened? That my father made you?'

'Him?' The child stretched out one faintly translucent hand, and pointed at Mariana's father. 'Yes. I think I remember. But I remember other things too. I remember *you*. I don't know how.'

'It's difficult to explain.' Mariana stroked one honey-brown glass curl, and sighed. 'Papa made you to look like my little sister, Eliza. She died. Six days ago. Everything has felt wrong, ever since. We miss her – especially her mother, you see? Papa was trying to make something for her to love. She *will* love you, I'm sure she will. But anyway, when Eliza was dying, Papa caught her last breath, in a glass bubble.'

'Yes. That's inside me.' The child nodded. 'Is that why I remember?' She frowned, delicate glass furrows appearing on her forehead. 'Am I Eliza, then?'

'I don't know.' Mariana swallowed. 'I just don't know. I don't think Papa does, either, that's why he's frightened. He's never made anything like you before. He's the greatest glassmaker on Murano, everyone says. He makes pictures and ornaments that move; that's not so special. But you can talk! And think – you must be able to think, if you're talking, mustn't you?'

'Yes. But I don't think I can be her,' the glass girl said decidedly, shaking her head so that her glass curls rang again. 'I can see some pictures inside me that Eliza saw, that's all. I know things – that you are Mariana, and you'll watch over me. And he is Papa, and they are Rafa and Giorgio, and they'll carry me piggyback if I beg.'

Giorgio laughed. 'Ask me nicely, Eliza.' Then he frowned. 'Are we calling her Eliza? Shouldn't we give her another name? Perhaps we should ask the mistress.' He nodded towards the house, and Mariana sighed. The glass child was Mama's, not hers. It was Mama who would be holding her, and fussing over her.

'Giorgio's right,' she murmured. 'We should dress you. Let's take you to Mama.'

CHAPTER FIVE

'ELIZA...' MARIANA'S STEPMOTHER PUSHED herself up from the couch, her eyes widening, and then filling with tears. 'Oh, Eliza, my sweetheart. I knew it, I knew it, you came back to me...' She reached out her arms, tears now pouring down her face. 'My little Eliza, you look so well. So healthy.' She was wound in the blankets that she had used to wrap Eliza, and now she plucked at them feebly, trying to free herself to reach her baby.

The glass girl wriggled in Mariana's arms, reaching

out herself. She called, 'Mama!' in her ringing voice, but Mariana held her tight.

'That's Mama, yes. But – wait a moment… Papa, should we say something?' She turned back anxiously to look at her father, but he was leaning against the counter, looking exhausted. 'Papa! We shouldn't have done this, not without warning Mama first. She thinks it's Eliza back again,' Mariana hissed to him. 'You have to tell her!'

He hardly seemed to hear her. Rafa and Giorgio were holding him up – the creation had drained him completely.

'You tell her,' Rafa murmured. 'The master can't do anything, Mariana, you'll have to explain.'

Mariana set the glass girl down behind her. 'Stay there, just for a minute. I have to explain to her,' she began, but her stepmother had finally freed herself from the blankets, and was staggering forwards. She'd hardly eaten over the last week, and she was in as bad a way as Mariana's father, feeble and tottering. But she clearly didn't care. Her face was transformed by a great, shining joy.

'Mama, it's not Eliza. Please listen – Papa made her for you. She's like Eliza, but Eliza can't truly come back, you know that.' She caught at her stepmother's sleeve, trying to hold her back, to make her listen, but her stepmother brushed her away like a fly. Mariana saw that she hadn't even heard. All her attention was on her baby. She had no time to listen to Mariana – she probably hadn't even seen that she was there. She collapsed on to her knees in front of the glass girl, who was standing in the middle of the shop, staring back at her doubtfully now. 'You came back,' she whispered.

The glass child looked up at Mariana, leaning anxiously over them. 'Did I?' she whispered, taking a step back from the woman's reaching hands.

'No... Not quite. She thinks you're the old Eliza, you see. It's because she's so sad. I should have explained first – we were so excited for her to see you.'

'Eliza?' Bianca quavered, still holding out her hands. 'Eliza, won't you come to me, baby? You've been away so long. Where did you go?'

'Oh…' Mariana whispered, her own eyes filling with tears now. 'Oh, Mama. Eliza's gone, she can't come back.' She pulled at her stepmother's shoulder. 'Mama, remember. Eliza – died.'

'No.' Her stepmother shook her head. 'No, I thought so too, Mariana, but look, she's there. We were wrong.'

'I'm not Eliza,' the glass girl whispered, faltering. 'Papa made me.'

Shaking her head, Mariana's stepmother reached out one hand, and stroked the glass girl's cheek. 'Cold…' she whispered, drawing her fingers back, her voice full of horror. 'Oh, Eliza, no. You have come back. Mariana, she came back too late. A ghost!'

'She isn't.' Then Mariana stopped uncertainly. Perhaps she was? Was that what Eliza's breath had done, created a solid little ghost? She didn't know. 'She's made of glass, Mama,' she tried to explain. 'Papa wanted you to have her, to comfort you.'

'A ghost!' Bianca wailed. 'My own Eliza, come

back as a ghost to haunt me. Oh, I can't bear it!'

'Why is she screaming?' the glass child whimpered, retreating into Mariana's arms. 'Doesn't she like me? I remember her so well – Eliza loved her.'

'Someone fetch the priest, oh, oh…' Bianca threw her arms up into the air, and slumped to the ground in a faint.

'Whatever's the matter with the mistress?' Lena came running in, drawn by the commotion. She shoved her way past the apprentices and crouched down by Bianca, patting her hands, and calling her gently. 'What did you do, Mariana?' Then, sharply, 'What is *that*? Oh, my life, sir, what have you done?'

'Don't be angry with her!' Mariana hugged the glass girl tightly. 'Papa just wanted to give Mama something to love. We thought she'd be happy.'

'Couldn't he have gone to the market and bought her a greenfinch?' Lena snapped. 'Is it any wonder she collapsed, seeing her dead baby walk towards her? Haven't any of you any sense? What have you done, sir?' she demanded sharply again, looking up at the glassmaker. 'You boys, help me get her upstairs. And him, too, I suppose.'

'What shall we do?' Mariana whispered, as Rafa picked up her stepmother and began to climb the stairs, and Lena and Giorgio half-pushed, half-carried her father after him. 'What about us?' she called shakily, but the shop was empty, and her little glass sister was huddled in her lap.

'You could come with us,' Mariana's father suggested again. He twitched uncomfortably at the tight collar of his best shirt, and sighed. His wife was curled in the corner of the couch again, clutching the blankets. She wasn't looking at her husband, but at Mariana and the glass Eliza, who were standing behind him. 'Come with us, Bianca,' he pleaded. 'I'm nervous, standing up in front of the Council. Come and stand next to me.'

She said nothing, just kept on staring. Eliza turned her face away, pressing it into the skirts of Mariana's best pink linen dress. Mariana's stepmother hadn't touched the glass girl again since that first meeting a week before, or even spoken to her. She had folded away into herself, not eating, hardly sleeping, just huddled up in the back of the shop. Mariana's father had even put a screen across the corner. He said that he wanted her to be able to grieve in private, but Mariana thought it was more about hiding her from the customers. Gossip had already spread about the glass girl.

'We might see the duchess, Mama,' Mariana said coaxingly. 'You know how we always went to watch, whenever she came to the church, or to bless the waters. You might see her close up. Maybe she'll even want to meet Eliza...' Her voice stumbled away to nothing. They had meant for her stepmother to say what the glass girl should be called, and as she hadn't, it had been harder and harder not to call her Eliza. Gradually, over the week, they had fallen into the habit.

Her stepmother flinched, and turned away from them all. Mariana sighed, glancing apologetically at her father. He patted her shoulder. 'Come on, then. Put your cloak on, Mariana, it'll be cold on the water. You too, little one.' Then he smiled at Eliza. 'Not that you'll feel it, I suppose.'

'I will wear my cloak anyway,' Eliza told him decidedly. 'I like it.' She swirled the dark red-purple wool around herself and pranced, sticking out her toes to admire her pretty stamped leather slippers. 'The duchess will want to see me, I think.'

Her father laughed. 'There's enough talk about you on the island, I wouldn't be surprised if it had spread to the city already. The duchess knows everything, they do say. Perhaps she's looking forward to meeting you.'

'Sir, the boy's here,' Rafa called from the doorway.

Eliza eyed him disapprovingly. 'Shouldn't those two be in their best clothes?' she whispered, pulling Mariana down so she could reach her ear. 'They don't look as nice as us.'

'Apprentices don't have a lot of money,' Mariana murmured back. 'I don't think either of them has another coat. At least they combed their hair.'

Leo was peering around the door of the shop, eyeing Eliza. Mariana had told him what her father had done, but he hadn't seen the glass girl yet. They hadn't taken Eliza out of the house, and Leo knew that Mariana's stepmother thought he was a bad influence, so he wouldn't come in.

Eliza leaned round Mariana to look back at him, and smiled. Leo swallowed, his cheeks turning greyish-pale under his layer of tan and dirt. 'I thought you meant she just looked a bit like Eliza,' he muttered. 'She's the very living image.'

'Living,' Mariana's father agreed. 'That's the meat of it, boy. That's why we've to go to the palace.' He pulled at his collar again. 'Who knows what they'll say?' He gazed down at Mariana and Eliza, and sighed, but then he twirled one of Eliza's honey-glass curls around his finger. 'You're a little marvel, whatever else you are. Whatever they say. Remember that.'

'I will.' Eliza stared back at him, her blue eyes

clear and wide. 'I'm not afraid.'

She was the only one who wasn't. The trip across the water and around the city was conducted in near silence, broken only by Eliza's delighted crows when a wavelet hit the boat, or Leo's oars flicked water on to her cloak.

They disembarked at one of the long jetties out in front of the Palazzo Ducale, and Mariana's father gave Leo a coin, and told him to wait. Then he set off up the jetty, under the bored, incurious gaze of the fisherboys and servants gathered around the edge of the water. Mariana followed him, Eliza's hand in hers, the glass smooth and cool. They passed without notice almost up on to the marble pavement, until Eliza stared too keenly at one liveried boy lounging in the stern of his boat, clearly waiting for his master or mistress to return from the palace. He glanced back at her, and then sat up all of a sudden, leaning over the side of his boat to stare.

Mariana flinched. She could almost feel that look. It was the first of many, she was sure. As they stepped on to the marble in front of the palace steps, she could hear the whispers starting to hiss behind them.

The footman at the door to the palace eyed them in the same bored manner, hardly bothering to let Mariana's father speak before he droned, 'Through there to the office and give your names to the clerk. You'll be called.'

'What does that mean?' Eliza demanded. 'When will we see the duchess? Does she have shoes as nice as mine?'

'No children,' the footman intoned, waving a lordly hand back out towards the water.

'She isn't a child.' Mariana's father twisted his tricorne hat between his hands. 'She's why we're here. She's a glass doll. I have to get the Council to look at her – the rules, you see. I think she might be one of those magical workings that has to be registered.'

The footman inclined his head slowly, as though his neck was stiff, and inspected Eliza, who was reaching out to touch the strings that bound the knees of his breeches. He stared at her slim, translucent fingers, and then at the guilty face she turned up to him when she realised he was watching. He coughed.

'Signor Cometti!' he called, still gazing fascinated at Eliza. 'Signor Cometti, I reckon this one needs to be taken to the Council Chamber...'

A fussy-looking man in black, with greying hair tightly pulled back, and a beak-like nose which gave him the air of some mournful water bird, popped his head out of the office. 'What? Half the city's in the waiting room, are you mad?'

'Look at her!' the footman hissed.

The clerk peered down at Eliza, who smiled hugely at him. 'I would like to see the duchess,' she explained, her thin, fluting voice echoing around the marble hall.

The old man bent down further, and lifted a pair of pince-nez spectacles, pressing them on to his nose and blinking at this strange sight. 'My dear...' he murmured. And then, 'Albert, is this child made of glass?'

'Yes, sir.' The footman nodded. He had lost a little

of his stiffness now, and he seemed to be trying hard not to look impressed.

'How very surprising. And she talks. Well, yes. Send a page up to the Council Chamber, Albert. Ah! Ahem.'

The footman and the clerk both suddenly straightened up, as though a great dignitary was passing. Mariana tried to look discreetly sideways, to see who it was. It could even be the duchess herself, or her cousin, Lady Mia. They must walk through the palace occasionally, after all. Though she supposed that they probably did avoid the entrance hall. She frowned. There was no one there.

'Oh!' Eliza slipped her fingers from Mariana's and pattered out across the streaked marble floor. Mariana grabbed for her, but she was already halfway across the room. 'What is it? Mariana, look!'

Mariana looked round at the clerk and the footman, not sure if she should go. It was a palace – she couldn't just go dashing off. But the pair of them were frozen, watching Eliza, and clearly weren't going to be any help at all.

'I don't know, I can't see,' Mariana hissed, hurrying towards Eliza. 'I don't think we're supposed to go this way…'

'But it's so beautiful! What is it, Mariana? I don't think Eliza ever saw this, I can't remember it.'

Looking up at Mariana with clear green eyes, eyes that had the same magical brilliance as Eliza's own, was a cat. A dark chocolate-furred cat with a jewelled collar. Hurriedly, Mariana bobbed her knees in a curtsey. She had never seen the cat before, but she knew exactly who he was – the whole city knew. Ten years before, when the Little Duchess had still been a child, she had made this beast for her maid Etta, out of a cup of spilled chocolate. His name was Coco. He too was a strange, magical creature. Perhaps that was why he had come to see Eliza. She was crouching down next to him, admiring the glitter of his whiskers, and as Mariana watched, she reached out to tap one. 'It's pretty, Mariana, look, I like it!'

'Eliza, he's special, don't touch,' Mariana

whispered, clenching her fingers into her palms so hard that the nails nearly cut her. But the little glass girl was patting the cat now, giggling delightedly – and he was purring back to her, nudging his nose against her hand. Then he walked away, just a few steps, before he stopped and turned back to stare at the two girls.

Eliza immediately went after him, and then came back with an irritated little grunt, grabbing at Mariana. 'Come on! He wants us!'

'You'd better follow them, sir,' the footman muttered to Mariana's father. 'The cat will take you to the duchess.'

'Now?' Mariana's father asked, rather feebly.

The clerk was pushing him after his daughters, flapping the pile of papers in his hand. 'Hurry!'

The glassmaker and his apprentices trotted across the marble hall and after the girls and the cat into a dim, wood-panelled passage. Mariana looked back in relief – she hadn't wanted to let Eliza run off on her own, but the thought of meeting the duchess had made her fingers feel colder than Eliza's. At least she wouldn't have to explain what her father had done.

The cat led them in procession through a series of passages. Mariana decided that they were meant for servants, since they didn't have any decoration, but they met no one. Perhaps the whole place was so huge and grand that the cat had his own secret ways around? The passages were very dark, so when they finally popped out through a side door into the hall of the Great Council, blazing with light and gilding and the fantastic costumes of the courtiers, Mariana stood there blinking on the threshold. Eliza had to grab her arm again and haul her on.

The walls and ceiling were covered in painted panels, framed in gilding so heavy it looked as though it couldn't possibly stay up. Mariana hunched her shoulders fearfully, and followed the cat along a slowly opening path between the knots of courtiers, leading up to a dais at the end.

Coco sprang lightly on to the lap of a young woman seated in the centre of the dais, wearing a yellow silk dress, and a thin gold circlet around her hair. She was already looking curiously at Eliza, and she smiled as the glass girl scrambled up on to the dais after the cat, ignoring all Mariana's panicked whispers to come back.

'He is very handsome,' Eliza said chattily, lolling against the duchess's lap and stroking Coco's ears. 'Is he yours?'

The entire crowd of courtiers had fallen silent now, staring at the strange child. Mariana could hear whispers: *Such smooth, clear skin. Quite odd-looking. Do you see her hair? And her eyes?*

'She looks like a painting,' one young woman close beside Mariana whispered curiously.

'He belongs to my maid,' the duchess murmured. 'But I made him.' She reached out to stroke Eliza's crisp glass curls. 'And who made you, little one?'

'He's a cat, isn't he? My sister said so. I hadn't seen one before. I don't know very much yet. Oh – my father made me. At least, he isn't actually *my* father. He was Eliza's father, and I'm not quite Eliza, though

I'm called Eliza too because I look so like her.'

'And this is your sister? And this your father – Eliza's father?' The duchess waved at Mariana, and her father, who was standing frozen below the edge of the dais, with the apprentices huddled behind him. Hurriedly, he bowed, an expression of panic spreading over his face.

'You made her, sir?' the duchess enquired, leaning forward. 'You're a glassmaker? From Murano?'

'Yes, your Grace,' Signor Galdini stammered. 'I came to report her to the Council, your Grace. I'd not made anything like her before. She's a living creature, you see. I hadn't quite meant this to happen. I was trying to comfort my wife – she was grieving for our younger daughter.'

'I'm so sorry – your daughter died?'

'Two weeks ago, and my wife, she won't talk, or eat. The glass girl was for her.'

'But she doesn't like me,' Eliza put in rather sadly. She was still playing with Coco's whiskers.

Mariana opened her mouth to say this wasn't true,

but stopped herself. Even Eliza, made of glass, and only a week old, could tell that it was.

'You're her sister?' the duchess asked, leaning forward. 'Come here, child.' She beckoned Mariana up on to the dais too. 'You look very similar.'

'Papa made her to look like the real Eliza, and we did look alike, even though we were only half-sisters. I think that's why my stepmother—' She halted. 'I think that's why the plan didn't work. The glass Eliza is *too much* like the real one. She makes my stepmother miss her more.'

'And how did your father enliven her?'

'With Eliza's last breath. He caught it in a bubble of glass, as a keepsake. This Eliza has it inside her.'

'I remember some things,' Eliza said, looking up from Coco. 'But not cats. Eliza was ill, she didn't go out often. I don't think she ever played with a cat.'

'Poor child…' the duchess murmured. 'Glassmaker – your name?'

'Signor Galdini, your Grace,' Mariana's father replied, bowing hurriedly.

'Signor Galdini. You were right to come to the palace, and show us this little marvel. Take the very greatest care of her. I pray that your stricken wife will recover, with the aid of her two excellent stepdaughters. I shall visit your workshop, next time I make the journey to Murano.'

'We shall be greatly honoured, your Grace,' Signor Galdini exclaimed, bowing again.

'Goodbye, little Eliza. Perhaps your father will make you a glass kitten to play with,' the duchess said, laughing and stroking Eliza's curls. The chocolate cat sprang down from her lap, stalking proudly towards the same side door, and they scurried after him.

CHAPTER SIX

'TRULY REMARKABLE,' THE PAINTER MURMURED, peering at Eliza. 'Such skill, sir! Would you do me the honour of touring your workshop? I have never seen glass made. There is some magic in my own work, of course; my paintings have been known to move, and even to speak on occasion, but this is truly wonderful.'

Signor Galdini led him out to the workshop, smiling broadly, and Mariana could hear them discussing pigments, and the magic of colour, as they crossed the little yard. Eliza sat down on the floor, with her feet stuck out straight in front of her, looking sulky. 'I am sick of being poked at,' she muttered, sounding so like the original Eliza after another doctor's visit that Mariana blinked.

'Didn't you like him?' she asked. 'Signor Felsi is very famous, Papa told me. He paints all the noble ladies and gentlemen. Don't you want him to paint you?'

'I don't care. All they do is talk about how clever your father must be, and what a great achievement I am.'

Mariana smiled at her. 'I know. It's because you're so beautiful.' She watched a faint pink flush run under Eliza's milky glass skin. 'It's true.'

'Is that why you like me?' Eliza whispered, glancing sideways at Mariana, her eyes a darker violet-blue than usual.

'No...' Mariana frowned. Why did she like the glass girl so much? She had adored her real little sister. So why didn't she find the glass Eliza impossible to love, the way her stepmother did? 'I don't know why it is,' she said at last, shrugging. 'Perhaps because I loved Eliza, and you remind me of her. You aren't all that like her though, except in looks. You're funny, and – and sharp. And you like *me*; that makes a difference. I like to talk to you.'

'No one talks to me except you. Everyone else just stares.'

'They'd be even more impressed if they did,' Mariana said soothingly. 'You talk like a little parrot, only better. Eliza was never so chatty.' Then she turned anxiously, looking at the screen across the corner of the room. It was so easy to forget that her stepmother was there. Mariana had tried so hard to tempt her out, offering her arm for walks along the quay, bringing her choice morsels of food. But Bianca hardly left her couch. Even though it had been two weeks since Mariana's father had made Eliza, his wife was no more used to the little glass child than she had been on that first day. She still hadn't touched Eliza, and she turned her head away whenever Mariana brought her near. Now Mariana was sure that she had heard a little catch of breath, a gasp. 'Mama?' she called gently. 'Mama, a great painter has come, did you hear him? He wants to paint Eliza, I'm to take her to his studio in the city tomorrow.'

'Oh… My baby….' A faint whisper floated out from behind the screen, and Mariana sighed. She beckoned Eliza to follow her, and slipped around the edge of the screen. Her stepmother was lying on the couch, her face pressed into the blankets. A smell of stale clothes rose up to meet them, and Mariana fought back a grimace. Eliza was peeping around the side, not daring to follow her.

'Mama, please,' Mariana whispered. 'Can't I fetch you something to eat? Or help you upstairs to change your dress?' She beckoned again to Eliza, scowling at her fiercely when the little glass girl shook her head. 'Look, Mama. She's worried about you.'

'*She…?*' Bianca sat up suddenly, fighting the blankets away. 'That! That is an abomination, a cruel joke on your father's part. Heartless and cruel. Take it out of my sight! It has nothing to do with my Eliza, nothing!' She lunged at Eliza, who jumped back with a scream, and scurried away out into the yard, to take refuge in the workshop.

'I am going upstairs,' Bianca hissed, gathering up the blankets. 'My Eliza's room. Do not let that creature come near me.'

'Signorina…' The painter bowed to Mariana, smiling. 'Are you admiring my work?'

'You painted the duchess!' Mariana turned to look at him, wondering if he had worn that same paint-splotched canvas smock while he was painting at the palace.

'I did. It was she who told me about your little glass sister, at our last sitting. She thought I would find her an interesting subject.'

'I wish I could paint,' Mariana murmured, hardly realising that she was speaking aloud. The duchess's face was withdrawn. There was a sense that the person standing in front of the painting might not be trustworthy, that she didn't yet know, and she was watching. It was eerie, and Mariana had seen it in her, when they went to the palace. A hidden, watchful intelligence behind her eyes.

'And why shouldn't you paint?' Signor Felsi asked. 'Your father has a great artistic talent, it would not be surprising if you had inherited it from him.'

Mariana whipped back round, surprised. 'You don't think it's wrong for girls to do that sort of thing? Paint or make glass?'

He gazed back at her, and his expression seemed honestly puzzled. 'Why ever would it be? Talent is talent.'

Mariana swallowed. He really seemed to mean it. 'Does everyone think the same way, in the city,' she asked slowly, 'or is that just you?'

He frowned. 'Most people, I would have said. I take it that your family doesn't agree?'

'Girls can't be glassmakers,' Mariana said, repeating the words she'd heard her father say so often.

'I know at least two women who are well-respected

painters,' Signor Felsi told her thoughtfully. 'Not many, I suppose, when there are men in their hundreds painting in this city, but they are there.' Then he smiled. 'If I had tried not to paint, I don't think I could have survived. My fingers draw without me thinking of it.'

'I draw in the sand,' Mariana confided. 'I go to the sea, in the evenings, and scratch patterns in the sand with sticks. That isn't really drawing, I know, but if I don't do it, my hands itch. But I thought I'd always have to pretend that I didn't. Or try to persuade myself to do something that was allowed. Like making lace, or embroidery.'

'The lacemakers do weave strong magic,' Signor Felsi pointed out. 'And I know of a girl in the city who embroiders spells.'

'Would you ever take an apprentice who was a girl?' Mariana asked him.

Signor Felsi frowned. 'I would have to think about it – if she had talent, I hope I would. But I suppose the truth is that her talent would have to be greater than a boy's.'

'But why?' Mariana demanded angrily.

He shrugged. 'Because it would be difficult. Unusual. I would have to find somewhere for her to sleep for a start – she couldn't sleep in the studio with the boys. And what would I do if she were to – er – fall?'

'You mean if she was going to have a baby?' Mariana scowled at him. 'You're as bad as my father. He told me a girl couldn't make glass in case the heavy work upset her delicate insides. What does he think scrubbing stairs is, or lugging around wet washing?'

'Perhaps…' He eyed her thoughtfully. 'Signorina, I came to ask, will you be in the painting too?'

Mariana blinked at him, too surprised to keep on arguing. 'Why?'

'You're very like your little sister. It will add greatly to the painting – the contrast between your natural skin, and the smoothness of her glass colouring.' He smiled. 'And I could give you paper scraps to take home with you, and charcoal. Better than sticks and sand, I promise.'

'Paper is very expensive...' Mariana said slowly. 'You'd really give it to me?'

'Like I said, scraps. Odd bits. Drawn on on one side, perhaps. Good enough for practice.' He smiled at her. 'If you're in the painting, you will have to come to the sittings. More time in the city. Away from the island...'

Mariana flushed, and pressed her hands against her cheeks. 'You see too much,' she muttered. 'I like to explore, that's all. I want to see things too. So much more happens here.'

The painter laughed. 'True. So will you come and sit for me? Is it a bargain? Time for paper?'

'Mariana, look.' Eliza had crept up beside them, and was pulling on her sleeve. 'The little dog in that painting turned to watch me. He did! He turned his head!'

Mariana looked over her shoulder at the painting. The piece was half-finished, the stretched canvas leaning up against the wall with a pile of others. She hadn't even noticed it – the studio was so full of paintings. They covered the walls, drawings spilled out of folders, creaking shelves held more piles, along with a collection of strange, unconnected objects that Mariana had at last worked out were props for the painter and his students. She had admired a large vase stuffed with dusty peacock feathers, and then seen the same feathers in the painting of the young woman that was propped behind the door – she wasn't wearing much else.

The dog was a small, sharp-faced little thing, painted in the very corner of the picture, almost as if he was about to jump out of the frame. The young woman who was the main subject of the painting looked as though she wanted to shout at him to come back and stop being silly, but she couldn't because she had to keep still. Just as Mariana was thinking this, the dog wagged his tail at her, and tilted his head cheekily.

'You're right,' she told Eliza. 'He definitely moves.

You said your paintings moved sometimes,' she added, turning back to Signor Felsi. 'I didn't know if you meant it, though. I didn't know paintings could do that. Do they all move? Will we?'

He smiled at her. 'I don't know. Most of my works do, but not all, by any means. It partly depends on the sitter. The duchess, for example, she does not. Or not that I've noticed so far.'

'She might when you're not looking,' Eliza agreed, pattering over to stare at the duchess's portrait. 'Maybe she doesn't want anyone to see where she goes.'

'I'll move her,' Signor Felsi suggested. 'You two come and sit on this chair for me, and I'll move her painting behind my easel so you can see her. You can watch to see if she moves,' he told Eliza coaxingly.

'Very well.' Eliza nodded. 'I think when you paint me I shall definitely move. Why would I want to stay still in a frame?'

Mariana groaned a little as she wriggled her feet – they'd gone completely to sleep, and she'd probably fall over if she tried to stand up. She should stop. But she couldn't, not just yet. It was almost, almost right.

'What's the matter, Mariana?' Eliza looked up from the silvery fish. Bianca had abandoned him downstairs in the shop when she moved to her daughter's old room, and the fish was the glass child's favourite pastime, just as he had been for the real Eliza. 'What is that?'

'A drawing…' Mariana sat up at last, blowing strands of hair off her forehead so as not to get charcoal all over her face – her hands were covered.

'Like Signor Felsi's?' Eliza asked excitedly, running to see. 'Oh… What is it?'

Mariana sighed. She had been kneeling on the floor, trying to draw all the strange pictures she saw in her head, but charcoal was so dusty and dark and grey. The paper was precious and wonderful, so much better than scratching in the sand, but now she was envying Signor Felsi his paint. She wanted colour.

'They were meant to be flowers,' she sighed. 'but flowers don't come in black and white.'

'I can see that they're flowers,' Eliza assured her, screwing up her face heroically. 'No, I can. Yes. Petals, like those flowers you picked to put in Mama's room.'

There was silence for a moment, hanging uncomfortably between them.

'She'll grow to like you,' Mariana said at last. 'It's only that she spent so long trying to care for Eliza – the other Eliza,' she added hurriedly. The little glass girl didn't seem to mind that she was only meant to be an imitation, but Mariana knew she'd hate it, if it were her. She tried not to talk too much about her sister in front of her replacement. Somehow, the glass Eliza seemed less and less like her sister every day. She was a peculiar mixture, oddly old and young at the same time. Her strange ways of seeing the world made her look foolish one moment, and deeply wise the next. Mariana could never tell which she'd be. 'Mama was so desperate to make her better,' she said at last. 'I know you don't see it, but she was so loving. Everything was about making Eliza well again – and now she has nothing.'

Eliza trembled a little. 'No. Nothing would be better. She has me, instead.'

'Don't say that,' Mariana pleaded. 'It isn't your fault.'

'I know.' Eliza drooped, fiddling with the folds of her lilac dress. 'But it still hurts me here. I have pictures of her inside me, from the real Eliza. Mama loved her so much. I want her face to look like that for me, and it never does.'

'Oh, Eliza.' Mariana knelt up and threw her arms around the glass girl, pressing her own warm cheek against Eliza's cool one, and hugging her tight. 'I love you.'

'Mariana!' Eliza squeaked, a few seconds later. 'Look!' She wriggled out of Mariana's arms, crouching down to stare at the drawing, and Mariana looked down too. 'Did you do something to it?' she gasped, watching as the petals unfolded from the grey smudges on the paper into petals, and buds, and then a trail of grey-black leaves. The two girls gazed open-mouthed as a faint wash of colour seeped up out of the paper, threading through the flowers as they opened out into a spray of pink blossoms, each one crowned with a puff of green-gold stamens. They were real – alive, the petals fragile and beautiful against the grubby paper.

'It wasn't me!' Eliza gathered the spray of flowers into her hands and cradled them, shaking her head. 'I can't do anything like this. There's magic in me, but it's Papa's, not mine. I can't use it. This was you!'

'But I only wanted to be able to draw,' Mariana whispered. 'Really draw, like Signor Felsi. Or to make glass like Papa and Rafa and Giorgio. I wanted to use the magic inside me to make something beautiful. I don't know what this is… I didn't even do it. It just happened.'

'It's your magic!' Eliza danced around the room, waving the flowers. 'And how can you say it's not beautiful? You're so clever, Mariana, just like Papa!'

'Ssshhh, don't tell him,' Mariana giggled. 'I'm not allowed. Oh, Eliza, ssshhh, he's coming!'

'Where did you pick those?' Papa had come into the shop, wearily stripping off his apron, and now he was staring at the flowers in Eliza's hand.

Mariana jumped, her eyes widening in panic. She didn't want to tell her father. She didn't know what had happened, but it was bound to be like glassmaking, something that girls weren't allowed to do. She stared at Eliza, her mouth moving with nothing to say.

'They're very pretty, I've not seen anything like them before. I hope you didn't steal them off someone's balcony, little one.' Papa leaned down to sniff the flowers, and stroke Eliza's hair.

Eliza shook her head, looking uncertainly at Mariana. 'No.'

Mariana swallowed, wondering what Eliza would say if she lied. The little glass girl was growing to understand the strange manners of the world she'd been brought into, the way it worked by promises, and half-truths and smiling lies, but she had little patience for it. Mariana had taken to hustling her out of the shop when customers were rude or sharp to Rafa or Giorgio, or Lena if Papa had sweet-talked her into minding the shop. Eliza refused to understand that customers had to be petted and coaxed into buying things, and she would answer back if they made comments about the glass.

'They were on the quay,' she said slowly, staring hard into Eliza's eyes, and then turning to smile at her father.

'Just growing out of a crack in the paving stones,' Eliza added. Then she glanced back at Mariana, her expression saying, *Aren't I clever?* but it made Mariana's heart ache a little, that she'd taught the little glass girl to lie. 'Aren't they pretty? Can we put them in one of the little vases?' She picked up a bright *millefiori* bottle.

'No, no... Honestly, child. Not that one. Something plainer. Here.' Her father brought down a soft green glass bowl. 'Trailing out of this, very pretty. Put them on the counter. Now, Mariana, listen. Will you go to the city for me? I have commissions coming out of my ears, I can't spare the time to go myself, but I want to give your mama a present. Something pretty to cheer her up.'

Mariana bit her lip, looking sideways at Eliza. Papa's last present had gone so badly. Her father saw the glance, and sighed. 'Yes... She must come out of her strange mood soon, surely?' he said pleadingly.

Mariana stared at him. His little daughter had died only three weeks before, but he seemed to have forgotten his love for Eliza already. Did he really think that a present was going to cheer his wife up, however beautiful it was? Her stepmother was long past that. She was like a ghost herself, and she was starting to frighten Mariana. Lena had been whispering about it at the market, too, Mariana thought. Or perhaps it was Rafa and Giorgio. She had seen the sideways glances from their neighbours.

'She needs a distraction. I thought perhaps you could go to that magician who made the silver fish for Eliza. Ask him for some pretty toy. A bird, maybe?'

A bird. Mariana ducked her head, so as not to look at him. He thought he could buy his wife out of her misery with a pretty bird. Sometimes, she wondered at her father. His work was so beautiful – it was almost as if all the best parts of him went into the glass.

'You're going to the city to sit for Signor Felsi again this morning, aren't you? Could you visit the magician after that?'

A smile of relief twisted at Mariana's mouth. The magician! She should have thought of it before – she had almost forgotten him, in all the strangeness that had happened since Eliza's death. Yes, Signor Nesso would understand about the flowers. He would be able to tell her what she had done – and, perhaps, what else she might be able to do.

Besides, the longer they were away from the shop, the better, Mariana thought. When her stepmother had lunged at Eliza two days before, when the painter had first come to visit them, it was as if she had moved into a different sort of grieving. She no longer lay on

Eliza's sofa, but stayed shut away upstairs in her daughter's old bedroom. She had locked the door, and wouldn't let anyone in, not even her husband. Lena left her meals outside the door, but she told Mariana that Bianca wasn't eating enough to keep a mouse alive. Mariana had tried knocking, but her stepmother didn't even answer. There was a deep, listening silence inside the room, and that was all.

Every so often though, Mariana had felt the hairs rise up on the back of her neck – as though someone was watching her. Or perhaps, watching Eliza. If she turned quickly, she could just catch a flutter of black skirts, as her stepmother disappeared back up the stairs.

It would definitely be better if they were out of the house.

CHAPTER SEVEN

'CAN'T WE GO BACK?' ELIZA asked, a faint whine coming into her pretty voice. 'We sat still for so long at the studio, I want to go home.'

Mariana huddled the hood of Eliza's cloak up around her shining glass curls, looking sideways at the passers-by. She didn't want a crowd – it frightened Eliza when people jostled around her. Besides, Mariana was too tired to fight off another auction. On their way to the studio, two court nobles had seen Eliza throw back her hood to watch the seagulls, and they had both demanded the right to buy her, bidding absurd amount of gold against each other, and ignoring Mariana when she tried to explain that the glass girl was not for sale. In the end, it had taken Eliza herself, shrieking like one of the sea-birds, to make them listen. Mariana had told them shakily that her sister was not for sale, that the duchess had forbidden it. That wasn't entirely true, but Mariana didn't think the duchess would mind.

She pressed Eliza close against her side, stepping in the shadows. She still wasn't sure how fragile her little glass sister really was, either. Would she break if she were knocked over? What would happen then? Mariana wasn't sure if Eliza could be mended, like her old doll.

'We're just going to visit a friend,' she explained to Eliza. 'It won't take long. I want to ask him about what happened.' She leaned down to whisper in Eliza's ear. 'With the flowers. Look, I brought one with me, wrapped in my handkerchief.' She showed

Eliza the little bundle, tucked away safely in the basket Lena had given them. She had packed up some bread and a little glass-stoppered jar of honey, so Mariana had something to keep her going through the portrait sitting. Eliza had stuck a finger in the honey – she could taste its sweetness, even if she didn't really eat.

'Oh!' Eliza brightened. 'Who is he? Is it Leo?' She liked the fisherboy – especially since he had told her about the giant squid that had apparently wrapped its tentacles around his boat and attempted to strangle him, last winter. Mariana had heard about the squid before, but knowing Leo she reckoned it might have been a middle-sized octopus, nothing more.

'No, silly. Leo lives on the island, like us. This is Signor Nesso. He's a magician, with a shop in Piazza San Marco. He made your little silver fish – do you remember, I told you about him? How he made the fish from my thoughts? That little fish is the closest thing I've ever seen to you, a living magic. I think he might be able to tell me what happened with the drawing. And we have to ask him for a present for Mama, too.'

Eliza nodded, now quite resigned to another expedition. 'The shop with the little golden birds?' she asked hopefully. 'Will we see them?'

'Maybe. I'm sure there'll be something to see. It's this way.' She hurried Eliza past the church of San Moise, tugging her gently as she stopped to gaze into the window of a maskmaker's shop, and then along an alley lined with luxurious shops on either side. Eliza trailed from her hand, cooing admiringly at the bright windows, and Mariana cast worried looks at the shoppers, hoping no one realised what her pretty little sister really was.

The alley led under the arches straight into the Piazza, and Mariana shooed her into Signor Nesso's shop at last, sighing gratefully.

'You didn't let me stop and look!' Eliza complained indignantly. 'I want to look at the hats!'

'Signorina! The young signorina with the fish!' Signor Nesso struggled up from behind the table at the back of the shop, smiling at her. 'And you've brought your Eliza with you. Was the medicine nice, little one? Did you like the taste of the berries? You look very well on it.'

Eliza stared at him, and Mariana bit her top lip. She hadn't thought – of course he wouldn't know. He had never seen the real Eliza, and in the dim light of the shop, and with Eliza's hood up... 'This isn't...' She coughed, and tried to start again. 'This...'

'Oh, my dear. Have I said something I shouldn't?' Signor Nesso came closer, peering at them both anxiously. 'I am so very sorry, child.'

'How could you know?' Mariana shrugged helplessly. 'My sister died...' She counted in her head, looking at the dusty ceiling. 'Nearly three weeks ago. My father made Eliza – this Eliza – out of glass.'

'Glass?' Signor Nesso leaned down, wheezing a little, and Eliza laughed at him, showing tiny, pearly glass teeth.

'You creak!' she said, giggling.

'I do indeed… You, my dear, are a little marvel. You talk!'

'I am a little bit the old Eliza,' she explained. 'Her last breath is inside me. May I please see your golden birds?'

'Of course you may…' The old man shook his head admiringly. 'Though they are not nearly as special as you.' He reached down the little black velvet bag from a hook attached to a shelf, and drew out the six golden feathers that Mariana remembered. He tipped them into his hand and blew on them, the breath curling out from between his lips tinted gold. At once the golden birds twirled upwards, spiralling out into the shop and twittering excitedly.

Eliza twittered too, squeaking and dancing and clapping her hands as she ran after the pretty creatures, and Mariana and the old magician watched them, laughing.

'You came here for more than just the birds, child, I can tell. Something bundled down inside you. Something frightening – no, perhaps not.' He frowned at her. 'Something different.'

Mariana put the basket down by her feet, and pulled out her handkerchief, unfolding it to show him. 'Yes. Both.' The flower shone in the faded linen, still fresh, the petals bright.

Signor Nesso took it gently, stroking his finger across the fluffy stamens and unfolding the layered petals a little further. 'This is no natural flower. Where did you find it?'

'I drew it,' Mariana told him huskily. 'Signor Felsi, the portrait painter, has been painting Eliza and me. He gave me some paper and charcoal, and I was trying to draw. I've always liked to, but I'd never had real paper before. I was cross, because I couldn't get the flowers to look right, they were too grey and flat. And then they weren't.' She nodded to the flower in his hand. 'It grew out of the paper. I don't know how.' She swallowed nervously. 'I did magic.'

'You did, you did. Very unusual, clever magic. Could you draw anything and have it come alive, I wonder?'

'I don't know!' Mariana lifted her hands, and stared down at them, shrugging. 'I don't know how I did *that*! I didn't do it – it just happened.'

Signor Nesso nodded. 'Yes… I remember the feeling, from when my own magic first started to show.'

'What did you do? Did you make things?' Mariana asked eagerly. 'How old were you?'

'I was ten.'

Mariana looked him up and down, without even thinking about it. Signor Nesso was so old and bent – had he ever been her age? Then she flushed scarlet, realising how rude she must seem.

He smiled at her expression. 'Hard to imagine, yes. I started to be able to understand people's thoughts. Much as I do now, but it was harder then. I didn't know what was happening – none of my family had any magic, not as far as I knew, and I was bewildered. So much of what I heard was ugly, and strange. I hated it, for a long time. Then one evening as I was sitting by our kitchen fire, I heard my mother, worrying about me. She was frightened – I was so miserable and angry, she worried what was going to happen to me. She was even worried that I would run away, or worse. And I had considered it – until I realised that I couldn't run away from something that was inside me. Twice, I stood at the edge of the canal, wondering if it would be easier to dive in and swim, and then just keep swimming until I was too tired to go any further.'

'What did you do?' Mariana whispered. She had been unhappy, wishing that things were different, but she had never thought of drowning herself.

He laughed. 'She was remembering the year before – before all the strangeness. How I had been such a happy, greedy little boy, always after honey cakes, or begging her for a handful of raisins. I remembered it too. I was so angry, suddenly. It seemed desperately unfair, that the little boy I was had been taken away from me.' He smiled into Mariana's worried eyes. 'Then I found that there was a honey cake in my hands.'

'You made a honey cake out of nothing! Did you eat it?'

'Yes. I gave half of it to my mother, and I ate the other half. It was very good. Then my mother brushed the crumbs off her dress, fetched her shawl, and bundled me out to see the old woman that everyone in our neighbourhood went to for spells, when the rats were too much to bear, or a young wife was praying for a baby. She took me on, not so much as an apprentice, more an errand boy. She taught me the little she knew, and then sent me to another magician, who knew a little more... And so it went on.'

Mariana nodded. 'I need someone to teach me, then.' She looked up at him, sideways, hopefully.

'You do. But surely you'd be better learning from your family? Your father is a great magician.' He nodded towards Eliza, now leaning against the table next to them, with the golden birds perched on her shoulders and nibbling at her glass curls. 'Look at what he's made.'

'He's spent so long telling me that I can't be a glassmaker,' Mariana murmured. 'I don't know what he'll say to this. What if he says no? And besides, I want to make your sort of magic. Spells that actually do things. My father's glass is beautiful, but there's so much more I could learn. Do you think I could?'

'I can teach you.' He sighed. 'But not without your father's permission. Talk to him, Mariana. You can't hide your magic, I promise you, it won't work.'

Mariana nodded. Perhaps that was true, but she still couldn't imagine telling her father that she could draw magic. Not with everything at home already so strange. 'I'll try,' she murmured. 'Oh! I forgot – he sent me to ask you for a gift for my stepmother. Something pretty to cheer her up.'

Signor Nesso looked doubtful. 'Well, I suppose we can try. A grieving mother, though…' He glanced along his shelves, frowning. 'One of these?' He lifted down a basket full of soft, striped silk scarves, and pulled one out to show Mariana.

She stroked the pink silk between her hands,

laughing at the softness. 'It's so pretty. So soft! Is that the magic?'

The old man shook his head, smiling. 'No. Wrap it around your neck for a moment.'

Mariana twisted the scarf over the collar of her dress, wondering what would happen. Then she laughed, pressing the silk against her nose. 'Roses!'

'Yes. And the purple ones smell of lavender. Would your stepmother like it, do you think?'

Mariana bit her lip. 'She ought to. It's beautiful – I'll definitely take it. She's so strange and sad, now, though. I don't know if she'll even want to put it on.' She sighed, and glanced out at the piazza through the arches. 'Oh, it's late. We should go – my father hired a boatman, and he'll be waiting.'

'Talk to your father,' Signor Nesso told her again, and Mariana nodded, wondering inside how she ever would. What was she going to do? Could she keep trying her magic on her own? Was it dangerous? What if she made something awful by accident? Mariana wound the pretty scarf around her hands, and knew that she didn't have a choice. There was magic inside her now – she couldn't risk letting it die away.

She huddled Eliza close on the boat trip home. It was cold and windy out on the sea, and the boat rocked unpleasantly on the choppy little waves. Even though Eliza couldn't keep her warm, she was still comforting to hold.

'Why aren't you saying anything?' Eliza asked, peering up at her at last, as the island eased towards them out of the autumn sea mist.

Mariana leaned closer, whispering. 'Signor Nesso would teach me magic, but only if I have permission from Papa. I'm not sure Papa will let me. He wants me to marry into one of the other glassmaker families – that's what he thinks girls should do. He doesn't listen to me, you know he doesn't. He always thinks he's right.'

'Get married, instead of making your own magic?' Eliza squeaked indignantly.

'Ssshhh. Yes.'

'That's stupid.' Eliza frowned. 'Couldn't you tell the old man that Papa said yes?'

'I suppose. But I don't want to lie to him. I want to be an apprentice properly! Why shouldn't I be?'

Eliza leaned against her arm and sighed gustily. 'I don't know. I thought it was one of those things that I don't understand.'

'I don't understand either,' Mariana growled. 'All I can do is keep on trying by myself. But I'll never learn properly that way.' They sat huddled together as the boatman drew into the canal between the houses, and the water smoothed and settled, the boat rocking gently as he pulled in to his mooring.

'Thank you,' Mariana called, as they climbed out. 'We'll see you again soon – when Signor Felsi sends word for us to come to the studio again. Goodbye!'

'Goodbye!' Eliza chirruped, waving, and they hurried along the quay towards the Vetrario Galdini. Mariana was hoping to catch her father in one of his free moments to show him the scarf, and she was hungry for some supper too. She'd beg something from Lena, she thought, perhaps some of the sardines the cook had preserved in oil the day before.

But as they pushed open the heavy wooden door of the shop, a figure loomed up above them, and Mariana stumbled backwards, almost knocking Eliza over. 'What – what is it?' she cried, recognising her stepmother after a few frightened seconds. She caught her breath. 'I thought you were – I don't know what. Something awful.' Then she swallowed hard, remembering Bianca's angry outburst, and the dark, shadowy presence she had been in the house, these last few days. Her stepmother's eyes looked so strange now, dark and glassy.

'Mama, what are you doing?'

Her stepmother had been wearing a black dress since Eliza's death, and now she had swathed herself in layers of black shawls too, so she looked like some great, flapping crow.

'You should go back to bed,' Mariana said, her voice still wavery with fright. 'You're shaking. Mama, please, you don't look well.'

'Nothing is well,' her stepmother hissed. 'How can I be well, when Eliza is gone, and this – *this* is in her place?' She shot out one thin hand, and grabbed Eliza's wrist. 'This thing has stolen my little girl's clothes!' She shook Eliza to and fro angrily, and the little glass girl squeaked in panic. 'And that's not all. She's taken you all in, hasn't she? So clever! Worming her way inside all your hearts! Not mine, you little minx.' Suddenly she lunged, trying to fling Eliza down on to the stone pavement.

'No!' Mariana shrieked. 'You'll break her, stop it!' She darted in, reaching to grab Eliza back, but her stepmother was quicker, snatching Eliza close and kicking Mariana away.

'What's happening? I could hear shouting from in the workshop! What's going on?' Mariana's father came hurtling out of the side passage, followed by Rafa and Giorgio, both looking eager for any sort of distraction from work.

Bianca turned to her husband, her eyes brighter now, as though she'd come back to herself. She smiled at him sweetly, still hugging Eliza close. 'These silly girls,' she murmured. 'Little Eliza was far too close to the water's edge. She was about to fall in – poor little thing, she doesn't understand. I had to shout, to warn her.'

Mariana's father looked at his wife doubtfully for a moment, and then at Mariana, who was crouching against the wall of the shop, rubbing her leg. Mariana could tell that he didn't believe what his wife was saying, but clearly he couldn't bring himself to call her a liar.

'Mama is tired,' she whispered shakily. 'I think you should help her back upstairs to lie down. I'll look after Eliza.'

Her father prised his wife's fingers from Eliza's arm, and the little glass girl ran to Mariana, flinging her arms around her sister, and burying her face in Mariana's cloak.

Mariana watched fearfully as her father led her stepmother back into the shop. Her stepmother was looking back over her shoulder, still with that sweet, eerie smile.

'She tried to break me,' Eliza whispered. 'Didn't she? She tried to throw me down and break me.'

'Yes.' Mariana hugged her tighter. 'But I won't let her hurt you, I promise. I'll keep you safe, Eliza, always.'

CHAPTER EIGHT

IT WAS STRANGE HOW TIRING it was just to sit still in the painter's studio and be stared at, Mariana thought, when she woke up the next morning. The sun was well up, and golden light was streaming through the cracks in the shutters. She was sure she had slept very late, and she wondered why Eliza hadn't woken her. The glass girl didn't seem to need sleep in the same way she did. Eliza closed her eyes as if she were sleeping, and lay down next to her, but she never seemed to be deeply asleep. She always woke

Mariana in the mornings, eager to be up, either out wandering along the canal, or watching Papa and the boys in the workshop, or bothering Lena in the kitchen. She did all the little-girl things that the real Eliza had struggled with.

Mariana blinked sleepily at the huddle of blankets next to her, and realised that Eliza wasn't there. She had gone downstairs on her own, then. A tiny cold lump of fear settled in Mariana's stomach, and she flung off the bedclothes, snatching at her skirt and bodice, which lay on the wooden chest at the end of her bed. She dressed hurriedly, and then ran downstairs, darting first into the shop. She was hoping to find Eliza dancing in the patches of sunlight that poured through the windows and lit up the shelves of glass, but there were only tiny specks of dust twirling in the light.

'Lena, have you seen Eliza?' she demanded, bursting into the kitchen.

'No.' Lena was busy kneading dough, and didn't look up at her – she kept her eyes fixed on the bowl.

Mariana backed slowly out of the kitchen, into the yard, the cold feeling growing in her stomach. Lena knew something, she was sure. 'Mama was in Eliza's old bedroom upstairs,' Mariana whispered to herself as she ran across the yard to the workshop. 'The door was shut. I'm sure she was in there. And Eliza knows to watch out for her now. She wouldn't have let Mama get close.'

In the workshop, Giorgio and Rafa were making the glass canes that would be sliced to make *millefiori* flowers – the sort of job that her father could leave them to work at on their own.

'Where is he?' Mariana panted. 'Where's Papa? Have you seen Eliza? I can't find her.'

The boys exchanged glances, and said nothing. Rafa shrugged.

'What's happened?' Mariana slapped her hand down on the marble slab, and Rafa snarled, 'Watch it! You'll burn yourself!'

'Tell me what's happening!' Mariana yelled at them.

'The master went out, with little Eliza. That's all

we know, Mariana.' Giorgio patted her arm. 'She's perfectly safe.'

'But why didn't he tell me? I could have gone with them. There's something not right.' Mariana looked between them, her heart thumping in quick, sickening beats. 'Something awful's happening. I know it…' She turned slowly, and saw her father standing in the doorway of the workshop, a weary expression on his face. He was quite alone.

'What have you done?' Mariana whispered. 'Where's Eliza? What's happened?'

'She's gone.' Her father busied himself taking off his good coat, and brushing non-existent dirt from the hem.

'Gone? What do you mean? Did Mama…?'

'No, no. She's safe, I promise. But she's gone.' He dropped the coat over the back of the glassblower's chair and caught Mariana's arms, holding her tightly and looking her straight in the eyes. 'I've kept her safe. She'll be well looked after – and no one will hurt her.'

'You mean you've taken her away from Mama!' Mariana cried. 'But what about me? I need her...'

'Think about what nearly happened yesterday,' her father said wearily. 'Your stepmother is...' He shrugged helplessly. 'I made a mistake. It was stupid of me, and now I'm paying for it. I was grieving for Eliza too, and I thought I was helping your mama. I wasn't – I was distracting myself with the magic, putting all my memories of Eliza into the glass.' He straightened his shoulders. 'Now I've paid for my mistake. We should go back to remembering the real Eliza. Your mama was right – the glass child was a deception. A lie. I should never have made her, and we're better off with her gone.'

'No!' Mariana shook her head fiercely. 'You can't say that, you mustn't! She's beautiful! She doesn't stop me missing the real Eliza, I love both of them, don't you see? Where have you taken her? You have to tell me!'

Her father shook his head silently, and Mariana felt her fists clenching. 'If you don't tell me where she is, I'll go back to the palace and ask to see the duchess. She told me to look after Eliza. I'll tell her what you've done!'

'Don't be a fool. The duchess wouldn't see you.' But he looked a little worried.

'She would! You know it – she loved Eliza. The duchess was the one who told Signor Felsi he should paint her. She'll make you tell.' Mariana had never stood up to her father like this before, but anger was bursting out of her. She couldn't bear to think of Eliza, frightened and confused, perhaps alone. It was too cruel.

Her father folded his arms, standing straighter. 'I sold her to Count Renigo. As a gift for his little daughter.'

Mariana's mouth fell open; she stared at her father, aghast. Even Rafa and Giorgio seemed shocked. She heard Giorgio mutter, 'Sold her?' and Rafa let out a low whistle of surprise.

'He wanted her,' Signor Galdini said defensively. 'They'll take the best care of her – she'll be like a little princess in that great house. You can't tell me she'd be better off here!'

'She *belongs* here! What if the Count's daughter breaks her? Don't you remember? She broke a platter, didn't she?'

'An accident,' her father mumbled. 'Nothing will happen to Eliza. She's safe there.'

'What will you do with the money?' Mariana demanded bitterly. 'Will it tide you over until you can sell me? That's what you mean to do, isn't it? You'll arrange some advantageous deal – with old Signor Sillani, is that what you're thinking? Are you marrying me off to his son? I've seen them staring at me in church, you know, I'm not stupid! Eliza wasn't yours to sell, don't you understand? She belongs to herself! She's real. And so am I!' She was screaming now, shouting it into his face, and her father was actually flinching back from her. Then he seemed to pull himself together. He grabbed her shoulders, and shook her hard.

'You're hysterical, girl. Be quiet!'

'I won't! I won't!' Mariana wrenched herself out of his grip and darted out of the workroom and down the passage. She raced out on to the quay, panting and shaking, wearing only her old, everyday clothes, with not even a cloak, or a bag. No one followed her – probably her father thought he'd gone too far, he was leaving her to stew, thinking she'd come creeping home in an hour or so.

Mariana looked up at the shop behind her uncertainly, crossing her arms over her chest at the chill in the air. Her things – should she go and fetch them? She turned away, shaking her head. She would not go back. All she needed was Eliza. She was going to fetch her sister. After that, who knew where they would go? Anywhere was better than here.

'I still don't see how you're going to get Eliza back,' Leo said, panting a little as he heaved on the oars. 'What, you're just going to walk in and take her? Count Renigo bought her. He's not going to give her to you.'

'He can't buy her. She wasn't Papa's to sell,' Mariana growled. She had an old sack that Leo had found in the boat huddled around her shoulders against the cold. It stank of fish, and it wasn't improving her mood.

'Good luck convincing the count. Do you even know where the Palazzo Renigo is?'

Mariana blinked. She hadn't thought of that. 'No. Do you?'

'No!' But then Leo sighed. 'Oh, very well then. I do. I've sold fish there. It's a great, grand barn of a place, Mariana. I've only ever been to the kitchens. But you can't go there, Mariana. I don't think they'll take kindly to you marching in and demanding Eliza back.'

'I know,' Mariana whispered. 'But I have to try! What do you want me to do, just leave her there? She won't understand what's happening. I'd bet anything Papa didn't explain what he was doing, or why. He doesn't think she's a person, the way we do. She's just one of his creations, like the dancing glass frogs he made that everyone loved last year at Carnival time. A special little novelty. He doesn't understand that she's real, even though he knows he put part of the old Eliza inside her. Will you take me there, Leo, please?'

Leo muttered to himself, but he nodded. 'You won't get in, I'm telling you now.'

They drew up to the entrance of the Palazzo Renigo in a swirl of damp mist. The building towered over Mariana, the heavy black iron doors forbiddingly shut. Leo tied off his boat to one of the striped mooring poles, and folded his arms, staring at her. 'Go on, then.'

Mariana shook off the sack, wishing that the smell of fish hadn't transferred itself on to her too, and climbed out of the boat, slipping clumsily on the weed-strewn steps.

'Watch it!' Leo reached out to steady her, but she shook him off.

'I'm not going to fall!'

'Suit yourself. Do you suppose the count's going to

send you and Eliza home in his personal gondola? Or shall I bother waiting?'

'Yes, please.' Mariana's voice went small as she looked at the barred doors, and the grand carved frontage. 'I have to try,' she said again, and Leo nodded. 'I know.'

The door creaked open, and a tall manservant in a powdered wig stared down at Mariana. 'What are you hanging about on the steps for?' he snapped. 'Be off.'

'I'm not hanging about.' Mariana's voice came out as a quavery whisper, even though she was trying to shout. 'I've come to see the count.'

'You?' The manservant goggled at her. 'Get out of here.'

'I'm a representative of the Vetrario Galdini!' Mariana squeaked. 'I have important business with the count. He'll want to see me, you'll get in trouble if you don't let me in!'

'Get off these steps, you little hooligan. Go on! Out of here!'

Mariana stepped back. She could see that he was never going to let her in.

'And good riddance!' the man snapped, as he slammed the door.

'Don't say *anything*,' Mariana warned Leo, as she climbed back into the boat.

'Wouldn't dare. Where are you going now, though?' He leaned over to untie the boat.

Mariana sighed. 'I don't know. I haven't anywhere to go. I won't go home, not without Eliza. I've got to find some way to get her back, but how?' She huddled the sack around her shoulders again. 'Could you take me just a little further down the Grand Canal? So I can cut through to the Piazza? I'll ask Signor Nesso for help – he said he'd teach me. Perhaps he'll let me sleep on the floor of the shop.'

Leo looked at her doubtfully. 'Didn't he say he needed your father's permission to teach you? What if he sends word back to Murano?'

'I don't think he'd do that.' Mariana drew her top lip between her teeth. 'Maybe he would. I don't know.

What am I going to do? I shouldn't have stormed off in a temper. I should have gone back and packed my things, at least.'

'No.' Leo shook his head. 'If you'd done that, I reckon you'd never have gone. Better to make a clean break.' He was silent for a moment, still rowing. 'What if you went to the back entrance, where I go to sell the fish?'

'But that's not going to help me get Eliza back,' Mariana objected.

'You're not going to get her just by asking, though, are you? You'll never be allowed in to see the count, and even if you were, they'll say they paid for her, fair and square.' He shipped the oars for a moment, the boat slowing almost to a halt among the busy water traffic. 'You'll have to steal her back.'

Mariana stared at him.

'It isn't stealing anyway, bearing in mind what you said about Eliza belonging to herself,' Leo pointed out. 'And I reckon it's the only way you're going to get her. I'll take you to the kitchen entrance, and say you're my cousin, after a job. Grand places like that, they always need maids, don't they?'

'Do they?' Mariana nodded eagerly. 'That's brilliant.'

Leo smiled at her, and then suddenly he shook his head. 'No. It would be, except that that stuck-up beanpole in the wig's just chased you off the front steps. Confound it. He'd recognise you, straight away.'

'Do you think so? He only saw me for a minute or so...'

'Mmm, but it's his job to guard the house from undesirables like you. He'll remember.'

'I wonder...' Mariana sank her chin on her hands. 'Do you think he'd know me if I looked different – maybe if I had different-coloured hair?'

Leo shrugged, and then yelled at the boatman whose gondola had nudged too close. 'Don't know. Maybe not. We need to get going, Mariana, one of these idiots will have us sunk if we stay here any longer.'

'It's all right, just take me to the edge of one of the alleys. I can cut through to the church of San Moise. Signor Felsi's studio is round there.'

'What, that painter?' Leo frowned, pulling over to the side of the canal. 'What do you want him for?'

Mariana beamed at him as she scrambled out. 'I'm going to get him to paint my hair!'

'This is my cousin, Signora,' Leo explained, bowing humbly to the housekeeper. 'I wondered if there might be work for her here. She can clean, and cook a little.' He ignored Mariana's worried glance. She had watched Lena, but that didn't mean she knew how to cook herself. But this was the only way she could think of to get close to Eliza. Surely if she was in the same house, she'd be able to find some way of sneaking the glass girl out? What they'd do then, Mariana didn't know. She couldn't imagine going back to the Vetrario. Not after what her father had done. And not with her stepmother hiding in the shadows, ready to smash her fragile little sister.

Mariana twisted her hands together miserably, realising that she felt safer here, in this strange, damp basement kitchen, than she did in her own home. It wasn't her home, not any longer.

'We have enough serving maids,' the housekeeper said, looking Mariana up and down rather dismissively. Signor Felsi had mixed up a painted spell, as Mariana had hoped, turning her hair a much darker shade of brown, and he had given her a little white cap, and an old shawl that had been lying around the studio. She looked more respectable than she had when she'd approached the front doors of the palazzo. 'She's far too young,' the housekeeper said, shaking her head. 'What are you, child? Nine, ten years old? You should be at home with your mother.'

'My mother's dead, Signora,' Mariana said pleadingly, dropping a curtsey.

'Hmf.' She eyed Mariana, and asked again, slowly, 'How old are you, child?'

'I am ten, Signora.'

'I don't need any maids, not as such… But perhaps

you could be useful. The little daughter of the house, Signorina Julia, is without a nursemaid at the moment. She can be...mischievous. A respectable young girl such as yourself to wait on her could be a good influence, perhaps.'

Mariana swallowed, remembering Julia racing off across the bridge, and nodded, trying to smile. 'I would do my very best, Signora,' she promised.

CHAPTER NINE

MARIANA HAD EXPECTED THAT SHE would have to see the countess before starting work as Julia's maid, but it seemed that all the decisions about the palazzo's staff were taken by the housekeeper, Signora Raccagna, who was some sort of poor relative of the Renigo family. From what Mariana could gather from the gossip in the kitchens while she ate, the countess spent most of her days consuming elegant and luxurious meals, or lying on a couch in her withdrawing room, with her maid anointing her temples with eau de cologne. In between, she went shopping.

Once she had finished the bowl of soup Signora Raccagna had given her, Mariana followed her up the stairs to Julia's rooms. 'Now, should you meet one of the family on the stairs or in the passages,' the housekeeper instructed, 'you are to stop, and draw to the side, looking down at the floor, do you understand?'

'Yes, Signora.' Mariana nodded, thinking how very different it was to home. They had Lena to do the cooking, and they sent the washing out to Leo's mother, but Mariana and her stepmother had always done most of the cleaning between them. From the way Signora Raccagna was talking, the Renigo family would never even pick up a dropped handkerchief. Mariana was amazed they didn't have staff to feed them their dinners.

She wound her fingers nervously in her white apron as they approached Julia's room, and Signora Raccagna scratched politely at the door. Eliza would be in there, and Mariana wasn't sure what to do. She desperately wanted to snatch her little glass sister and run, but she didn't know the house well enough yet. It felt as though it would take days to understand where all the different passages and flights of marble steps led. She would have to bide her time.

'Julia.' Signora Raccagna nodded politely to the younger girl, who was sitting at a white-and-gilt table in the middle of the room. The table was laid for a meal, with delicately painted china, all child-sized. There was a dish of little cakes, and a glass carafe of some sweet cordial, but this was a game, Mariana realised. China dolls were seated on the gilded chairs around the table, with plates in front of them. Julia was pretending to hold a party.

'My dear, this is Mariana.' Signora Raccagna waved at her, and Mariana stared at her feet. She should have told Leo to give her another name – Julia had met her at the glassmaker's. But Mariana was almost sure that her stepmother hadn't told the count and countess her name, and Julia hadn't asked. 'She is to be your personal maid.'

Julia looked round, apparently surprised. 'Why? I've never had a maid before.'

Signora Raccagna seemed to suppress a sigh. 'Your mother and I have not been able to find you a nursemaid, or a governess. Mariana is close to you in age; I thought she would be good company.'

Mariana saw a faint twitch of a smile at the corner of the girl's mouth, and wondered if Julia's past nursemaids had gossiped about the child after they'd left. Perhaps the job was known as one to avoid. She wondered if Julia threw things. But then Julia stood up, and she saw that there was another doll drooping miserably on the chair right next to her. A doll almost life-size, dressed in a grand, lilac silk dress, with an expensive piece of lace veiling her glass curls.

It was all Mariana could do not to run to Eliza, who was gazing at her anxiously, and shifting on the chair as though she would like to leap up too. She pressed a finger to her lips, and then smiled, and Eliza smiled back and nodded.

'What are her duties?' Julia asked, eyeing Mariana thoughtfully.

'To keep your rooms tidied and dusted. She will carry up your meals, help you to dress...'

'I see.' Julia nodded. 'Yes. Thank you, cousin, for engaging her for me.' She looked meaningfully at the door, and Signora Raccagna thinned her lips. But she still went, dropping the slightest hint of a curtsey to her young relative.

Mariana waited, her hands folded neatly in front of her apron. She hadn't disliked Julia that much when she had taken her to the church, apart from thinking that she was irritatingly spoiled. Clearly her mother and the servants gave her whatever she wanted in order to keep her quiet. But being at her beck and call all day – and probably all night too – was very different to amusing her for an hour or so.

'You look familiar.' Soft little footsteps padded around Mariana, and she dared to look up, a polite, questioning expression on her face. She couldn't stare at her feet for ever.

'My lady?' she murmured, trying to sound confused.

Julia was staring at her suspiciously. 'You do! But I can't see why.'

'Perhaps I remind you of someone else, my lady?'

'I suppose that must be it.' Julia whisked back to the table, and pulled one of the grand china dolls off her chair, casting her on to the floor. 'Sit there!'

Mariana shook her head. 'I don't think I'm meant to.'

'You're *meant* to do what you're told. Don't you know anything?'

Mariana swallowed, and sat down, smiling lovingly at Eliza on the other side of the table. Eliza leaned forward, clearly wanting to ask Mariana what was going on, and Mariana shook her head. She pressed her finger to her lips again as Julia fussed with the flask of cordial, and then mouthed, 'Later!'

Eliza sat back, but she was fidgeting unhappily, and Mariana wasn't sure for how long she would manage to keep silent. She realised that she didn't know what her father had told Count Renigo and his daughter. Did Eliza talk to her new owner? Did Julia even know that she could talk? So far, she seemed just to have been acting like a rather unusual doll.

'Why are you staring at her?' Julia asked sharply, sitting down and glaring at Mariana.

Mariana ducked her head. 'She's very beautiful, my lady. Is she made of glass?'

'Yes. My father gave her to me this morning. He bought her from a glassmaker. She moves, which is clever, I suppose...'

'Don't you like her?' Mariana tried to keep the shock out of her voice.

Actually, this was good. If Julia didn't like her new toy, perhaps she wouldn't be too worried if Eliza disappeared.

Mariana held back a sigh, staring down at her fingers. Honestly, how likely was that? Of course this spoiled little rich girl would make a scene – and when that happened, Mariana realised worriedly, the count knew exactly where her expensive toy had come from. He would go straight to their father, asking for a new glass girl. There would be no hiding Eliza, either, pretending that they didn't know where she was. The count would hear soon enough from the gossip around the city if the glassmaker's strange little creation had returned to him.

Mariana *could* simply steal her little sister back – but then that would mean they would never be able to go home. Mariana rested her shaking hands on the table. Even if she could bring herself to return home, they wouldn't be able to. They were shut off from her old life for ever. What were they going to do?

'She's supposed to be magical, but she isn't really that interesting. I have prettier dolls. But this one was a present from my father, which makes her special. Now pretend that you are a noble lady, coming to call on me,' Julia directed. 'I am Countess Renigo – that's my mother, of course.' She leaned back in her chair, elegant and languid, and put on a high, fluting voice. 'And of course, my daughter is *such* a trial to me...'

Mariana stared at her, and Julia sat up again. 'Well, say something! You aren't very good at playing, are you?'

'Um. Is she?' Mariana tried to imitate Julia's affected voice, but it came out as a squeak, and the younger girl laughed.

'Yes, she simply won't behave herself – another governess gone, can you believe?'

'What does she do to them?' Mariana asked, truly curious this time.

'I won't do anything to you,' Julia said, changing back to herself, and fluttering her eyelashes innocently. 'I promise. More wine, Lady Sofia? And how is your husband, has he recovered?'

The game went on for most of the afternoon, with frequent stops for Julia to tell Mariana how stupid she was being, while Mariana clamped her lips together, and darted pleading glances at Eliza when she could. They couldn't let their new mistress know who Mariana was. Eliza had to keep quiet.

Eliza scowled, but she said nothing, even when

Julia told her new maid that she was worse than useless.

'I'm sorry, my lady,' Mariana murmured. 'I don't know all this court gossip. I haven't any secrets to tell.' She ducked her head to hide a smile.

'Then make them up,' the younger girl told her impatiently. 'Just say that Countess Minivra has had her emerald necklace snatched out of her gondola by a giant octopus, it doesn't matter if it isn't true!'

'But it couldn't—' Mariana started to say. Then she sighed. 'I hear that the duchess is having her portrait painted by Signor Felsi,' she said, remembering something that she did actually know.

'Oh? He painted me, you know. But my husband said it was a dreadful likeness, and he refused to pay.' Julia giggled. 'And that's true. Signor Felsi's portrait kept sneezing every time Papa's cats walked past, just like Mama does. He sent it back. Oh, I'm bored with this game now.' She stood up, and ran to a tall cupboard against the wall. 'We'll play battledore and shuttlecock instead.' She pulled out two little wooden bats, with parchment stretched across their circular frames. 'Have you ever…? No, I suppose not. You have to hit this, look. This is the shuttlecock.' She held up a cork, decorated with feathers, and Mariana gazed at it dubiously. 'We have to keep it from falling to the ground. Well, come on!'

'In here, my lady?' Mariana asked, looking around at the delicate glass chandelier – she knew quite well how much those cost – and all the ornaments and paintings that filled the room.

'Of course.' Julia handed her a racket, and pushed her over towards the windows. 'You stand there. Now hit it back to me – up in the air, yes, like that!' She giggled, dancing about and waving her racket, and Mariana rushed to and fro, half the time trying to hit the little bundle of feathers, and half the time trying to shield the pretty china ornaments on the mantelpiece. Luckily, Eliza was well out of the way behind the table. Since Julia obviously couldn't care less about the ornaments, she had a distinct advantage, which Mariana thought was probably a good thing. If she played too well, the little horror might decide to throw a tantrum.

'Oh! That was much better than trying to play with my governess. She just used to stand there holding the battledore and squeak, like a little mouse.' Julia subsided on to a gilded sofa, puffing. 'Fetch me some of the rose cordial.' She waved at the table, and Mariana hurried over, taking the chance to clasp Eliza's hand and drop a kiss on her cheek. Eliza clutched her hand tightly back, and Mariana felt something inside her lighten, and she pressed her other hand against her lips to stop it bubbling out. 'I have to pour her a drink,' she whispered. 'Oh, Eliza, I'm so sorry. I can't believe he did this. I'll work something out, I promise. We'll talk when she's asleep.'

'Look,' Eliza breathed back, pointing at the glass that Mariana had picked up. It was an ugly piece, Mariana thought, too heavy on the gilding, and the net-like *reticello* pattern not properly even. But now the gold slathered around the rim and the stem of the glass was sliding away, pooling at the foot of the glass, and shaping itself into a tiny golden heart.

Mariana swallowed, wondering if this sort of thing was going to keep happening. She hadn't told the gilding to move – it had been her love for Eliza, spilling out of her. *I'll have to be careful*, she told herself. *I wonder what happens if I get angry?*

'Oh, do hurry!' Julia called crossly. 'I'm so thirsty!'

Mariana pressed the golden heart into Eliza's hand, and snatched up another glass, in case Julia noticed the missing gilding. She poured in the cordial and carried it to the sofa, placing it on a little polished wooden table.

Julia snatched it up and drained it greedily, then she lay back against the cushions, staring at Mariana. 'What shall we do now?' she murmured thoughtfully, and Mariana hid a sigh. She was already exhausted, and she understood why the nursemaids and governesses had left.

'I should tidy the room, my lady,' she murmured. 'Signora Raccagna said it was my responsibility to keep it neat. I'll be in trouble if I leave it like this.'

'But I want you to play with me.' Julia pouted. 'I'm bored. More battledore! Or chess, do you play chess?'

'No, my lady.' Mariana sucked in a breath through her teeth as Julia seized a wooden box from the cupboard, and spilled a glittering pile of jewelled ebony and ivory chessmen out over the table. The glass that she'd stolen away the gilding from toppled and smashed, and Eliza slid down in her chair, trying to keep out of the way.

'Oh!' Julia stamped her foot crossly. 'Clear it up. Sweep the pieces into the fire, or something, before I cut myself.'

'Yes, my lady.' Mariana swept the broken glass into the ash bucket, ready to take it away when she relaid the fire the next morning. The next morning – she would still be here. It was a strange thought. *We could just stay here for always*, Mariana said to herself. *We'd be safe, at least.* And then she shuddered. She wasn't sure how long she could stand Julia ordering her about. Besides, she could hardly practise her magic as a palazzo servant. Someone would notice, sooner or later, even if she had got away with whatever she'd done to that glass. She might not be so lucky next time. A few days, though. She could put up with the rudeness for a few days, while she and Eliza made a plan for the future.

Mariana curled up on the narrow bed outside Julia's dressing room with a grateful sigh. Today seemed to have lasted a very long time, from that first strange moment waking in the sunlight, through a long afternoon of battledore, and make-believe, and Julia's strange interpretation of the rules of chess. She had prepared her young mistress a bath, filling it with cans of hot water carried up the stairs by the youngest of the footmen, whose job it was to wait upon Julia. Then she had dressed her in her lace-trimmed nightgown, and drawn the heavy embroidered curtains around her bed, before she crept off to her own.

She lay there, trying to listen for the slowing of the

younger child's breathing as she slept, hoping she wouldn't fall asleep herself first. She was desperate to talk to Eliza, but she had been running about after Julia all day, and she was exhausted. The glass girl was piled up on the padded bench at the end of Julia's bed with all her other dolls – Julia would have to be properly asleep before Mariana could sneak in and take Eliza.

But then she heard a delicate padding of little footsteps, and in the faint light of the candle lantern by Julia's bed, she saw Eliza coming towards her. She sat up, gathering the glass girl into her arms, feeling the cool smoothness of her skin, and running her fingers through the stiff glass curls. 'She didn't see you go?'

'No. Oh, Mariana. I was so glad to see you. I didn't know what to do.'

'What did Papa say to you? Did he tell what he was doing?'

Eliza shuddered, and nestled closer against her. 'No. He told me we were going to the city, that was all. I thought he meant the painter's studio. I wanted to wait for you, but he said you were sleeping. Then when we got to the city, I told him we were going the wrong way, and he put his hand over my mouth. I tried to struggle and run away, and in the end he stopped, and I thought we were going back, but he said – he said I was a danger. That he should never have made me. He said that your stepmother's wits were wandering, and I was making her worse, and that she might hurt me, and you too, so I had to go.' She gasped. 'He said that girl would take very great care of me.'

'Her! She'd break you and never even notice,' Mariana growled. 'She has more toys than she knows what to do with. She's a horror.'

'Yes...'

'You don't think she is?' Mariana whispered. 'You saw what she was like all day!'

'She had someone to play with,' Eliza said slowly. 'Before you came, there was just her, and the dolls, and me. She talked to us. On and on, like she did to you, but we didn't answer. I wouldn't – I told your father, if he took me away from you, I would never speak again, never, never, never.' She huddled herself against Mariana's shoulder for a moment. 'But I almost gave in. She hasn't anyone at all.'

'Well, now she has me,' Mariana said grimly. 'I don't know where else we can go. They'll come after us if we go back home, do you see? I think the count must have given my father a great deal of money for you.'

'I don't want to go back there. I only wanted you,' Eliza murmured.

'We'll think of something.' Mariana yawned wearily. 'We must remember not to let her see what you really are. We must put you back before she wakes...'

Eliza nodded, smiling a little as Mariana's eyes drifted shut. Then she curled herself in a nest of blankets, and watched the moonlight creeping across the polished boards.

Mariana dragged herself out of bed at first light the next morning, blinking wearily. She had never woken anywhere except in her room at the glassmaker's. Even the maid's narrow cubbyhole here had a high ceiling, and a glimpse of beautifully carved shutters, and a corner of tapestry. Gasping, she remembered Eliza – what if Julia woke and saw that she was gone? But there was only a hollow in the pile of blankets. Mariana pulled on her skirt and bodice over the chemise she'd slept in, and tiptoed into Julia's room. Eliza sat stiffly in a pile of dolls, as frozen and lifeless as they were.

Mariana hurried back to put on her stockings and shoes. It was her job to make up Julia's fire now, and fetch her a can of hot water for washing. Should she wake the girl? She wasn't sure, it wasn't something that had been in Signora Raccagna's long list of duties. Mariana wasn't sure if there was anything that Julia had to be awake for. The footman had brought her a luxurious supper to be eaten in her own rooms the night before, but did she eat breakfast with the count and countess? She worried over it while she stoked up the fire, wondering if she could catch the footman and ask. But the hot water was already steaming in its jug outside the door, and she carried it in.

Julia was sitting at the end of the bed, staring at her, her arms folded and her lips thin. Mariana came close to dropping the jug. 'M-my lady?' she murmured.

'I remember. Murano. You're the glassmaker's daughter. You took me to see the church with the pretty floor, and the dragon bones. You've done something to your hair, though.' She frowned, and then suddenly reached out to grab Eliza from the bench at the end of her bed, snatching her up and staring at her. 'The glassmaker's daughter... The same glassmaker?'

Mariana said nothing, and Julia dropped Eliza, and scrambled down from the bed to stand in front of her. 'You have to tell me, if you want to keep your job!'

'Who says I ever wanted to be your maid in the

first place?' Mariana snapped back, suddenly angry instead of scared. This wasn't her fault! Why were she and Eliza the ones to suffer? 'Why would anyone want to be maid to a spoilt brat like you?'

'You can't talk to me like that...' Julia seemed to be truly shocked, and Mariana wondered if anyone had ever been rude to her before. She didn't mean to, but she laughed. Julia's indignant pouting face suddenly struck her as incredibly funny.

'You're laughing at me! Don't you dare!'

Mariana didn't realise what the little girl was about to do – she didn't even dodge. She simply gasped as Julia hit her open-handed across her cheek. Then Julia stepped back, cradling her hand, as though she had hurt herself too. She didn't seem to make a habit of hitting people, at least, Mariana thought dazedly.

'Don't hurt my sister!' Eliza screamed, struggling down from the side of the bed, and running to hammer at Julia with her hard little fists.

Julia screamed, though mostly from shock, Mariana thought, not because Eliza was particularly hurting her. She flattened herself against the silk bed-curtains, staring down at the glass girl. 'You can talk!' she whispered.

'Didn't my father tell you she could?' Mariana asked curiously, picking Eliza up and cradling her.

Julia shook her head. 'He only said that she could move, and to be very careful as she was breakable. So she's your sister?' Julia asked, creeping forward a little, curiosity overcoming her fear.

'Sort of,' Eliza explained. 'Her true sister died. I was made to comfort Mariana's stepmother – the original Eliza's mother, you see?'

'No. Why did your father sell you?' Julia wrinkled her nose. 'Are you very poor?'

'No, we are not!' Mariana snapped. 'He didn't sell her because we needed money. It was because she...made things difficult... He doesn't like it when things are difficult.'

'Why, then?' Julia came closer, staring up at Eliza in her sister's arms.

'Because it all went wrong. My stepmother wanted

her real baby, not a glass one. She tried to smash her. Eliza reminds her of the real Eliza too much. Do you see?' She sighed. 'I was so angry with him, but I suppose it was actually quite a clever thing to do. Eliza is safe here, protected by all your family's servants. Your father even has his own men-at-arms! She couldn't be better protected. It's true, Eliza.'

'I still hate it.' Eliza glared at Julia, who actually hung her head.

'Does that mean you're going to leave?' she murmured.

'I don't know. I don't think we can. Your father paid for Eliza – if she disappears, he will try to get her back. So I can't take her home with me, your father will come and get her, and he could probably have *my* father arrested.' Mariana shuddered. 'They could even say that it was some sort of criminal scheme, that my father had sold her and then sent me on purpose to steal her back.'

'Surely if you take her home to Murano, your stepmother will attack her again, as well,' Julia pointed out thoughtfully, reaching up to play with the pompoms on Eliza's little leather slippers. Eliza withdrew her foot, huddling closer into Mariana. But then she seemed to relent a little, poking out her toes and wiggling them at Julia.

Mariana eyed the younger girl. 'Yes. I think she would. We can't go back, you see. But I can't leave her here, either. Eliza belongs with me. Even if you bought her, and she actually belongs to you.'

'You needn't be angry with *me* about it,' Julia snapped, turning away and folding her arms. 'I didn't know.'

'I suppose not,' Mariana admitted. 'So, we can't go home. I don't know where else to go...' She looked pleadingly at Julia. 'My lady. If we ran away – somewhere – would you give us, perhaps a day and a night, before you tell your father we're missing? That would give us some time to hide. I could go to the painter who helped me change my hair. He might be able to disguise Eliza. We'd find some way to pay back the money, I promise, even if it takes us years.'

Julia snorted. 'I saw through your dyed hair almost at once. How is a painter going to disguise her? She's made of glass, anyone can see it.' She shook her head decisively. 'No, you'll have to stay here, both of you, while we plan what to do.'

Mariana gaped at her, and Julia shook her head crossly. 'No one is ever going to believe that you are a proper servant if you look like that! Close your mouth!'

Mariana obeyed, snapping her mouth shut, but staring at the younger girl with wide, troubled eyes.

'Don't you see? It's the only thing to do. As you say, you can't go home, and Eliza is safer here than anywhere else. You had better write to your father, to tell him that you're safe – otherwise he might search for you. And then perhaps we can find some way to make another glass girl, to stand in for Eliza so that you can run away... Is that possible?'

'I don't know,' Mariana whispered. 'You'd really do that for us?'

Julia shrugged. 'It's a lot more interesting than

following my mother round the dressmakers,' she pointed out. 'But you'll have to practise being a more convincing maid. If Signora Raccagna decides to engage another governess for me, everything will become a great deal more difficult.' She made a face, wrinkling up her rather long nose. 'I might have to pretend to be good for a while.'

Mariana spent a long time writing the letter to her father – trying to tell him why she had left. Trying to make him see that it wasn't worth begging her to come back, or storming up to the palazzo to demand that she return. Not that she thought he would make the effort to do that. Really, she decided, after at least five screwed-up drafts, what she wanted was to make him see that he had been wrong. But she was almost certain that he would never admit it. In the end, having spent three days scribbling at the letter every time she wasn't supposed to be doing something else, and constantly having Julia correct her spelling, and sigh over her handwriting, Mariana gave one of the pageboys the letter, telling him to find a boatman going to the island. She had to bribe him with a silver coin that Julia had given her, since the boy seemed strangely reluctant to go down to the quay. Mariana stood by the kitchen door, watching him go, the letter clutched in his hand. He edged down the alleyway, looking back over his shoulder, and then suddenly raced away around the corner.

Dear Papa,

I am sorry that I was so angry. I see now that you sent Eliza away to keep her safe. Even though I still don't agree, I understand that you were trying to protect her from Mama. I have taken a post as a servant to Lady Julia, Count Renigo's daughter. I am with Eliza, and I can take care of her.

I came here to the Palazzo Renigo four days ago, planning to steal Eliza back, but Lady Julia recognised me, and persuaded me that it would be safest for both of us if we were to stay here. Please do not attempt to make me come home. I cannot leave

Eliza. I know that you made her to stop Mama grieving, and in this she failed, but I think she has helped me to remember and love Eliza, exactly as you wished. I find I cannot be angry with you when I think of this, in spite of what you did.

I promise that I will take the utmost care of Eliza. Lady Julia is not as spoiled or unpleasant as I thought she was – at least, she is spoiled and unpleasant, but mostly she is lonely. I think Eliza is very good for her. Now that she has decided that she will speak to Julia after all, she spends all her time telling her off, and already I think Julia is a little better behaved.

With love,

Mariana

Leo brought a reply to Mariana's letter the next day. Her father's note was on a torn and splattered scrap of paper, the back of a design for those same green glass dancing frogs.

Mariana Dearest,

You must return home at once. I have told the boy to bring you back with him in his boat. I have been at my wits' end, with no idea where you were, or even if you were safe.

Everything is going from bad to worse – first the tragic death of my little Eliza, then your disappearance, and now your stepmother has also abandoned me. She left a confused message with Lena, from which I gather that she has gone to stay with her sister in the city. Perhaps this is a good thing, as it will give her time to grieve quietly in a house where she is not constantly reminded of Eliza. But I am left with only Lena and the apprentices; it is not good for my work.

'Your father does moan, doesn't he?' Julia commented. She was leaning over Mariana's shoulder, reading the letter. There wasn't a great deal of point trying to persuade her not to. 'If your stepmother's darling baby has died, he might be a bit kinder about her wanting to get away from the house where it happened.'

Mariana opened her mouth to protest, and then didn't. Papa did sound almost as spoilt as Julia. 'I suppose he does. He's quite selfish,' she said slowly. It was something she had had only begun to learn over the last few days. 'He's so very good at his craft, you see. Everyone does what he wants, most of the time.' Frowning, she went on reading the letter.

You must return at once, as I am bereft, without any of my family. My work is suffering. I cannot come and fetch you without the count seeing who you are, which would be disastrous – imagine the gossip, if a daughter of the foremost Vetrario in Murano was found to be working as a servant! The news might even get back to the duchess, which would be most unfortunate.

I will even undertake to show you a little of the glassworking magic, though I still very much doubt that even a daughter of mine would ever be able to work glass with any great skill.

'Oh!' Mariana screwed up the letter and hurled it across the room. Julia dived after it, so that she could read the rest.

'I am so glad that you told the boy you wouldn't go. Do you know, I think your father might even be more conceited than mine?' she said at last, wrinkling her nose. 'What is this about teaching you glassworking magic?'

Mariana sighed. 'I used to beg and beg for him to teach me his magic,' she explained. 'I have inherited some skill in magic from him – but only a very little, and I don't know yet what it will be. Nothing, if my father has his way. In Murano, girls are not taught magic. Not glass magic, anyway. That's only for boys.'

Julia sniffed. 'Are you supposed to marry, like me? I have decided that I never will. After all, Duchess Olivia isn't married, and neither is Lady Mia, so I don't see why I should have to. My mother says it's my duty to ensure that I have a son to inherit the family title, but as far as I can see that was her duty, and she didn't do it, so I don't think I should have to do it instead. Who cares if there aren't any more Count Renigos?'

Mariana blinked. She had never heard anyone else say such things – the things she'd always longed to say to her father. Perhaps it was easier if you had been brought up to think that you were special and noble, and most of the people in your house existed only to run around after you picking things up.

'Darling Mariana. Will you show me your magic?' Julia asked, leaning over the back of the sofa, and whispering in Mariana's ear. It was later that day, and the girls were in Julia's room, as they almost always were. Phrases from her father's letter were still running round and round in Mariana's head, and at first she blinked at Julia, hardly understanding her words. 'I don't know how to,' she tried to explain, shrugging a little. 'I've never done magic on purpose.

That's why I need someone to teach me – like Signor Nesso, the old man who has the shop in the Piazza that I told you about.'

'With the golden birds! Oh, Mariana, couldn't you make me a golden bird? I'm so bored!' Julia wailed. 'Come on, come down to the garden and make me a bird! Please!'

'I'll come to the garden,' Mariana agreed, putting down the box of dolls' clothes she had been sorting for Julia. 'But I can't promise a bird – I'll try. But I never know what will happen. I've only made flowers once, and the heart Eliza showed you.'

'And the glass tear in your necklace,' Julia reminded her, picking up Eliza, and wrapping her in one of the dolls' cloaks. 'That was your very first magic.'

Mariana smiled. 'Yes, I suppose it was.' She let Julia pull her out of the room and along the passage, down the great staircase to the courtyard garden. It was tiny, but full of sun, even on a wintry day. The water splashed and glittered in the fountain bowl, and there was a sweet smell of herbs.

Julia forgot the golden bird for a while as they raced in and out of the empty flower beds and round the fountain, but at last, when they sat panting on the marble rim of the fountain bowl, she caught Mariana's hand.

'Just a little bit of magic,' she pleaded. '*Something…*'

Mariana sighed. She could feel the power, deep down inside her – there to be called on. She had done nothing with it, not since the little heart she'd made out of her love for Eliza. Didn't Julia deserve something too? After all, she had kept their secret.

A drop of cold water splashed on to Mariana's hand, and she laughed at the sharp sting, shaking the droplet away on to the marble. Then she smiled, dipped her hand into the water and began to draw on the stone with her damp fingers, a faint image on the grey-white marble.

'Oh, what are you doing?' Julia whispered, and Eliza leaned over from her lap to look.

'A boat,' Mariana murmured, her voice dreamy. 'Sails catching the wind, and golden ropes, and a golden cargo, all for you...'

'Mariana...oh...it's real,' Julia whispered. 'Look at her, she's sailing across the fountain! A boat, for me!'

Mariana blinked, and turned round to look. The stone rim was dry, and sailing slow and stately across the fountain bowl was a tiny wooden ship, her sails all gold.

'You meant that to happen,' Eliza whispered. 'You drew a boat, and the magic made it real.'

Mariana nodded, speechless, looking between her fingers and the boat. It was nearing the edge now, and Julia picked it lovingly out of the water. 'Oh, it's heavy! Is there something inside it, Mariana?' She lifted up a little trapdoor and laughed. 'Honey drops! Golden honey drops! A golden cargo, just as you said.' She stroked the golden sail, and then eyed Mariana sternly. 'You have to go to that magician. That Signor Nesso. You must!'

'She's right.' Eliza slipped a cold glass hand into Mariana's. 'Somehow, we must.'

'Someone's coming.' Eliza skittered across the room, and jumped on to the sofa, leaning back rather stiffly like a doll. Mariana hurriedly got up from her chair, and sat down on a small stool at Julia's feet, picking up the scattered threads from Julia's embroidery basket (which she never used, except for playing cat's cradle).

Julia snatched up the embroidery – which Mariana had been doing, to while away the hours in the stuffy, scented rich girl's rooms – and bent over it studiously. There was a scratching at the door, and one of the pageboys opened it, bowing to Julia. 'The count sends his compliments, my lady. He has asked for the whole household to be gathered in the Grand Salon. At once.' He bowed again, and backed out of the room.

Mariana and Julia exchanged anxious looks. 'Do you think your father's found out I'm not a proper maid?'

'How could he?' Julia muttered. 'I haven't seen him since you arrived, and you've never seen him.' But she was plucking at the silver thread embroidery on her blue silk dress.

'Don't do that, you'll spoil it,' Mariana said automatically.

'And don't speak to me like that when we go downstairs, or everyone will know you're not a proper maid,' Julia snapped.

They glared at each other, and then Mariana sighed. 'I'm sorry. I forgot. It's just that Anna will have to restitch it if you pull the threads like that, and her sight's going.'

'Who's Anna?' Julia asked curiously.

'The dressmaker who comes in to mend your dresses… Don't you know any of the servants?'

Julia shrugged. 'How would I?'

'I suppose she never comes in here.' Mariana shivered, suddenly glad of the chance to leave Julia's rooms. The little girl was allowed to play in the courtyard garden, and she did occasionally go on visits or shopping trips with her mother, but most of the time she was kept in her own apartments.

Admittedly they were huge – a bedroom, a dressing room and a large salon of her own – but Mariana was used to running about the quays and exploring the beach. She had only been at the Palazzo Renigo for five days, and already she felt stifled, shut up inside. Their confined existence made it much harder to find a way to solve their problems, too. She had been hoping to visit Signor Nesso in his shop and ask his advice, but she wasn't sure how they would manage it, unless they somehow managed to persuade the countess Signor Nesso could cure her sneezing. 'We'd better go, if your father wants us so urgently. I wonder what it can be about.'

She walked demurely behind Julia down the marble staircase to the *piano nobile*, the first floor of the palazzo, which held all the smartest rooms, the ones that were shown off to guests. The ground floor did have the marble-clad entrance hall that Mariana had been shooed away from, but the rest of it was kitchens and storerooms and rooms for the servants. It was too close to the canal and too damp for grand living.

The servants were filing silently in, lining up along the walls. Mariana wondered if anyone knew why they were gathering – the room felt fearful, as though every person in it had drawn in their breath, and not dared to let it out.

The count had been sitting at a small table, writing, paying no attention to the silently waiting servants. Julia marched up to stand next to him, and put her hand on the account book he was writing in. 'What's the matter?' she demanded. 'Why have you sent for everyone?'

The count looked up, clearly surprised, and appeared to notice for the first time that all his servants were gathered, watching him. He laid down his quill pen, and smiled at Julia. 'I meant for your governess to come, Julia, not you.'

'I don't have a governess, Papa, she left, weeks and weeks ago. Don't you remember?'

The count turned to Signora Raccagna, who was

hovering anxiously a short distance away. 'Have we not employed another governess?'

'The countess was not sure that it was necessary,' Signora Raccagna murmured, obviously trying to be diplomatic.

'She means that Mama said there was no point, as the new one wouldn't last more than a month, so why should she bother?'

Someone in the ranks of servants tried to turn a laugh into a cough, and the count ran a thoughtful look along the lines.

'I have Mariana instead, Papa. She is a very good maid. Come here, Mariana.' Julia beckoned to her imperiously, and Mariana curtseyed to the count as well as she could while holding Eliza.

'Ah, and the little glass girl. Are you enjoying your present, my dear?'

'Yes, Papa, she's very pretty. Papa, when I had a governess, she would take me out for walks around the city. May I go with Mariana? I would like to take the air a little. The garden is stuffy and boring,

I'd much rather walk outside the house. Otherwise, I'm worried I might start to sneeze all the time, like Mama.' One of the count's cats peered up at Julia from underneath the table, and she giggled. 'You aren't meant to be here,' she added, reaching down to tickle the purring creature under his chin. 'Mama will be cross,' she warned her father, shaking a finger at him.

'They don't like to be shut up either.' Her father sighed. 'I don't know, little one. This is why I called you all together,' he went on, raising his voice. 'A strange figure has been seen outside the palazzo – as some of you may know.'

There was a tide of sudden whispering, lapping around the lines of servants, and Mariana frowned. She had spent most of her time in Julia's rooms – she even slept there now, on a little cot bed at the side of Julia's grand curtained one, in case Julia needed her in the night. But she did go down to the servants' quarters occasionally, to take messages for Julia, or to fetch her washing water, or if she had a sudden desire for a piece of fruit or a honey cake. That morning, Julia had complained of a sore throat, and she'd sent Mariana for a warm honey drink. She'd waited, warming herself by the huge kitchen fire. She enjoyed listening to the servants' gossip, and she was so much the youngest of the maids that if she was polite, she'd often be given a handful of dried fruit, or a corner of pastry. But the maids had hardly noticed her. Several of them had been gathered in a little whispering clump in the corner of the kitchen, and one of them had been sobbing, with her apron thrown over her face. At first Mariana had assumed that the crying girl had been jilted by one of the footmen, but she'd seemed frightened, not angry, and the others were muttering worriedly. 'What if he comes back?' she'd heard one of the maids ask. 'I have to go out to the market…'

'What's the matter?' Mariana asked the older woman making the tisane for Julia, but she'd only shaken her head, and thrust the cup into Mariana's hands. 'Don't let those silly girls scare you,' she murmured. 'Run along back to Lady Julia.'

Now it seemed that there was more to it all than kitchen gossip. Perhaps this was why the pageboy hadn't wanted to deliver her letter.

'No one is sure who this figure is,' the count went on. 'But he has clearly been lurking about for the last few days. We must all be on our guard. No going out except in pairs,' he told the servants sternly. 'And not after dark. If the countess or I intend going out in the evening, we will require a full escort, with torches.'

Mariana wasn't sure what difference that was going to make, when the count and countess only ever went down the front steps to their gondola, waiting on the canal. It was the servants who used the back entrances in their nest of snaking alleyways. Presumably this shadowy figure was a thief, waiting to pounce on a servant carrying money for the count, perhaps. She shivered, thinking of her stepmother, sneaking about in her black shawls.

'That is all.' The count waved a hand, languidly dismissing his household.

'Papa, does that mean that I can't go out?' Julia's voice was rather sulky.

Her father eyed her, and Mariana thought he actually looked a little nervous. Clearly he did not want to deny his daughter, and Mariana wondered what she had done when he'd tried it before. Julia was apparently known for the most dramatic tantrums, during which she kicked, bit, scratched and broke things. Mariana hadn't seen one yet, but the other servants had told her stories about them. As Julia's personal maid, she was much pitied by the other girls. She had been worried that they would be envious of her, living mostly upstairs, with only the lightest of duties, but it seemed that no one wanted to be in her place.

The count tapped his fingers together anxiously, and the cat leaped up on to his lap, staring arrogantly at the two girls. The count seemed glad of the interruption, stroking and fussing over the cat, until Julia snapped, 'Papa!'

'My dear, with this strange fellow lurking about,

how can I let you and your maid going wandering round the city?'

'Can't we go out in the gondola, then?' Julia suggested, leaning up against his arm, and opening her eyes pleadingly wide. 'Perhaps tomorrow. We could take a footman with us. Then if we feel like walking, we can disembark a little way from the palazzo – nowhere near this shadowy thief – and the footman can accompany us.'

'Oh, very well…' the count murmured, stroking Julia's dark hair. He looked rather surprised – almost wary, as if he was still expecting the tantrum to hit him any moment. 'Since you ask so sweetly, little one. But always with a footman in attendance, you promise me?'

'Of course, Papa.' Julia rubbed her head against his shoulder, just like one of his cats, and smiled at Mariana, her green eyes wicked. Mariana wondered how long it would take her to get rid of the poor footman.

CHAPTER TEN

'IT'S NONSENSE,' JULIA MUTTERED IRRITABLY, as they climbed into the Renigo gondola. 'Silly gossip. One of the maids has imagined some shadowy figure, and now everyone is fussing and panicking.' She glared at Daniel, the footman who had been sent to accompany them, and he stared stonily out across the Grand Canal, pretending not to hear her. 'Well, hurry up, then!' Julia snapped, leaning out from the little *felze* cabin, and waving at Daniel. He exchanged a meaningful look with Mariana as he handed Eliza to her, and hopped down into the boat.

'At least we're out,' Mariana whispered. 'I still don't understand why your father let you, after all this time. I've been here days and days, and you've stayed shut up in the palazzo the whole time.'

Julia fiddled with the fastenings of her cloak. 'But I suppose I never asked,' she admitted. 'I went out with Mama, or my governess, but never on my own. Not until you made me want to.' She looked at Mariana curiously. 'I suppose you went everywhere on your own?' she asked, her voice tinged with envy.

'It's different, on a small island,' Mariana pointed out, still whispering so that the footman didn't hear. 'And I wasn't ever wearing a dress that could probably feed a family for a year.' She nodded at the silver embroidery on Julia's silk skirts. 'But yes. It's good to be out on the water again.'

Mariana peered back at the palazzo as the gondolier cast them off, and plied the huge oar to move them out into the main channel of the canal. It was so beautiful, with stone garlands and the coat of arms carved across the front, and the delicate wrought iron balconies. The slatted wooden blinds of the *felze* made it hard to see, but as they drew further away, Mariana glimpse a faint movement in the darkness of the alley that ran down the side of the palazzo. She blinked, and craned her neck, trying to see better, but there was nothing more definite – just a thickening of the shadow, as if someone was standing there. She turned away, almost sure that she had imagined the figure – but the back of her neck was prickling, as if someone had been watching her.

'Lady Julia Renigo…' Signor Nesso bowed, rather awkwardly due to his stiff joints, and creaked upright again. 'I am most honoured, my lady.'

'Mariana says that you are a great magician, and you can make clever things,' the little girl announced, strolling around the shop and eyeing the jars and baskets with interest. 'But what I want to know is, if you are truly so clever, why are you not part of the duchess's court? She has all the best mages there to help her work with the water and keep the city safe.'

Signor Nesso smiled at her. 'My magic is not water magic, my lady. I create fancies, as Mariana has told you. Little, pretty things. I have what one of my previous masters called a butterfly mind.' He lifted his hand to his mouth and blew, and a rich velvet-brown butterfly, its wings spattered with blue dots, flapped idly towards Julia. It landed on her finger, and she laughed.

Signor Nesso leaned forward, peering at Eliza, who was wearing an embroidered cloak like Julia's own. 'Now, I had thought that you were another little daughter of Count Renigo, but I remember, he has but the one child. The little glass girl! Mariana, you brought her with you to your new position at the Palazzo Renigo?'

Eliza pushed back her hood, and smiled at him. 'She would hardly leave me behind, Signor,' she told him. 'But it didn't happen quite that way.'

'She brought me,' Mariana sighed. 'And that is

why we are here, Signor. We need your help. My father sold Eliza to Count Renigo, to keep her out of my stepmother's way. I ran away to rescue her, meaning to steal her back. That's why I'm working at the palazzo.'

'Should you be mentioning this in front of your mistress?' Signor Nesso raised his eyebrows at her.

Mariana blinked. She hadn't thought how strange it would seem. 'She's helping...' she explained, glancing round at Julia, who was laughing as the butterfly twirled around her head. 'I think she's bored,' she added to Signor Nesso in a whisper. 'It's an adventure for her.'

Signor Nesso followed her gaze, and sighed. 'She seems a sweet enough child,' he murmured. 'But I would watch that she doesn't lose interest. Who's to say she won't decide she prefers being the nobility rather than a conspirator?'

Mariana nodded. She didn't think he was right – but then Julia did keep surprising her, and she had been brought up in the strangest way. Her mother seemed to lurch between ignoring her for days at a time and then summoning her to be played with like a doll, and she hardly ever saw her father.

'I will,' she assured him. 'Signor, can you think of anything we can do? I will never be able to take Eliza home, not without my stepmother hurting her. As it is, she belongs to Lady Julia. It's wrong. We have to do something.'

The old man eased himself back on to a stool, and gazed at her thoughtfully. 'You must indeed. But my dear child, think – I agree that you don't want Eliza to stay at the Palazzo Renigo as a petted toy, and you should be learning your craft, not running after a spoiled child. But even if we can help your poor stepmother, and somehow placate the count, are you sure you actually want to go home?'

Mariana was about to reply that of course she did, but then she stopped, frowning. She had assumed that she wanted to go back to Murano, to her father. Even though she was still so angry and hurt by the way he had behaved, it was where she and Eliza belonged.

Except, if she went home to the island, her father might grudgingly show her a little magic. She would be married off to a boy she'd exchanged a few words with, nothing more, a boy she certainly didn't *like*. She hadn't considered that it might be best not to go back, that she could even be happier somewhere else.

'Let's not, Mariana,' Eliza whispered, gazing at her pleadingly. 'I don't like it there. Mama frightens me.'

It was like jumping off the quay into the canal. Mariana had done it a few times, dared by the boys, and she clearly remembered that strange moment of weightlessness, before you hit the water. Her stomach seemed to rise up inside her.

'What else can we do?' she whispered. 'We haven't anywhere else to go.'

Signor Nesso sighed. 'Leave me to think, Mariana. A few weeks ago I told you I couldn't take you as my apprentice without your father's agreement. It seems to me that I was wrong. Perhaps you would be better off here, learning to use your gift.'

Mariana caught his hand. 'Eliza? Would you take Eliza too? If we can find some way of freeing her from the Palazzo Renigo?'

He nodded. 'Is it worth the risk of speaking to the count?' he murmured to himself. 'I could offer certain magics in exchange for the release of the glass child.'

'You could cure my mother's sneezing,' Julia said, from beside him. She had the butterfly gently cupped in her hands. 'That would make my father happy – if he could let his cats roam the house, and sleep on his bed at night.'

Signor Nesso laughed. 'I can provide a remedy for the sneezing, my lady, but I can never make your mother enjoy the company of a cat.'

Julia giggled, but then her mouth twisted, and her voice came out as a growl. 'Mariana, what will I do without you and Eliza?'

'Visit them,' the old man said, smiling at her. 'It won't be long before Mariana can create you all sorts of pretty toys to fill your empty hours, my lady. You will be the envy of the city.'

Julia sniffed, and nodded. 'Yesterday Mariana made me a boat, to sail on the fountain in our courtyard. But it isn't because of the pretty toys that I'll be here every day. I shall be, I don't care what my father says. I'll be so lonely without you and Eliza.'

'A boat, my dear?' Signor Nesso looked eagerly at Mariana. 'Drawn the same way as your flowers?'

Mariana shook her head. 'In water, on the marble rim around the edge of the fountain bowl. '

'It floated all around the fountain, and when it came back to me, it had a cargo of honey drops,' Julia told the old magician proudly. 'I'm keeping it in my washing bowl for now, until we can sail it on the canal one day. Mariana, I think we must go back. Signora Raccagna said by no means must we stay out once it's dark, and look...'

The two girls looked out on to the Piazza, seeing the shadows gathering. Mariana sighed, and nodded. 'Yes, we must. Signor Nesso, we'll come back soon.' She clasped both her hands around his gnarled old fingers. 'I'm so grateful. You'll never understand.'

He laid his other hand on top of hers, and smiled. 'In a few weeks, my dear, when you've been practising your spells for hours on end, you'll wish you'd never set foot in this shop. I will only be doing what others did for me, many years ago. Now hurry home, all of you.'

'Where is Daniel?' Julia set her hands on her hips, gazing around indignantly. 'He was supposed to wait outside the shop!'

'I'll go and look for him,' Mariana said. 'He's gone to watch that juggler over there, I expect.' She set out across the Piazza, making for the busy little crowd watching the juggler. She was halfway there, hurrying between the knots of people, when a frightened scream brought her whirling round.

Julia was still in front of Signor Nesso's shop, but she was kneeling on the ground, clearly struggling to get up.

'What happened?' Mariana shrieked, racing back to her. Then as she pulled Julia up she added, in a voice flattened by panic, 'Where's Eliza?'

'He took her,' Julia gasped thickly, pressing a hand to her nose, blood oozing between her fingers. 'I'm so sorry, he hit me and I fell over, and then he was just gone!'

'Which way?' Mariana cast about frantically, and a young boy who was staring at Julia's bleeding nose pointed down through the archway out of the Piazza. 'He went down there!'

By now Signor Nesso had limped to his doorway. 'Mariana, what's happened?'

'Someone took Eliza! We have to find her.' Mariana tugged Julia after her, racing down the narrow passageway between the shops. She had been down here before, she remembered vaguely, with Eliza complaining because she wasn't allowed to look at hats. 'Where is she? Oh, where is she?' she panted, until Julia squeaked, 'There, look!'

A swirl of dark cloak had appeared ahead of them, darting out of a doorway and running on down the path. Passers-by turned in surprise to watch where the figure was headed, and clutched their bags and purses a little closer. A little figure was bundled underneath its cloak – clearly the thief had paused in the doorway to try and stop Eliza wriggling.

Mariana dashed after the cloaked figure, pounding on down the pavement, with Julia gasping and struggling beside her. She would have been faster without the younger girl, but she didn't dare leave her behind.

'Mariana!' Eliza had caught sight of them chasing her, and she redoubled her efforts against the thief, struggling against the thick folds of the cloak. 'Help me!' Her next words were lost, muffled in the woollen cloth as the thief darted down a narrow alley, one which Mariana thought must lead in the direction of the Grand Canal.

She hurled herself and Julia into the dark, stinking alley, slipping on the rubbish scattered over the muddy ground, and making for the line of faint light at the end, where the alley opened up into a paved bank beside a small canal.

It seemed that the dark figure had chosen the alleyway at random – Mariana could see him at the end of the passage, turning this way and that like a questing hound, trying to find the best way out. They had him! She flexed her fingers, thinking of drawing in the air, pulling out patterns, nets and ropes to trap him. She could do this, she had to. He would not get away – he would not steal her sister.

And then they came flying out on to the bank, and the cloaked figure turned back towards them with a snarl, the breeze from the water flinging back his hood. Bedraggled snakes of dark hair wound around the face, and Mariana fell back, gasping.

It was Mama.

That strange figure that had been lurking around the palazzo – it had been Bianca all along. She had found out where her false daughter had been hidden away. She had been waiting and watching for her chance to destroy the glass girl. She was going to smash her down upon the stones as she had always threatened.

Her eyes were dull and desperate, and her back was up against the wall. Eliza was pinned in her arms, fighting and scratching, and Mariana screamed, 'No!' as she saw what her stepmother was about to do. She plunged forward, reaching for Eliza. But her stepmother had already raised the fragile body high, and Eliza let out a high, terrified wail. Mariana snatched at Eliza's velvet cloak, trying to yank her away, and the fabric seemed to slip through her fingers. She grabbed, and grabbed again, but the little body was falling, and she couldn't catch her.

The noise seemed to go on for ever. A delicate, bell-like, crystal splintering, woven with a frightened scream. It echoed in Mariana's ears as she knelt weeping on the flagstones, gathering up as many of the glittering pieces as she could find. Eliza was gone – all over again. Both that last wisp of her sister, and the glass girl with her strange innocent ways, and her fierce loyalty and love.

Her stepmother stood there for a moment, the madness draining from her face, leaving it pale, and grief-stricken. She stirred the mass of crystal pieces with one foot, and then turned, hurrying towards the edge of the water.

Julia made a move to go after her, calling, 'No!' but she was nowhere near close enough to stop her. Bianca was marching with a purpose that Mariana hadn't seen since before Eliza died. She didn't jump, she simply walked on into the water, as if the greenish mass in the darkness would bear her weight. There was hardly a splash as she disappeared beneath the surface, no thrashing, or gasps. Mariana pressed her hand over her mouth, feeling suddenly sick. How could it be that easy?

Julia turned back from the water, and knelt down beside Mariana, her face streaked with tears. 'What are we going to do?'

'Nothing,' Mariana answered dully, shaking the glittering fragments from her fingers. 'Eliza's gone. Really gone, this time. And my stepmother too – what am I going to tell my father?'

Julia was silent for a moment. Then she said at last,

'We should pick up the pieces.' She winced at the sight of a tiny glass hand. 'We could wrap them in her cloak.'

'Why?' Mariana asked bitterly. 'It's just broken glass now. Don't you understand? There's nothing of her left!'

'I don't believe that.' Julia shook her head, then winced at the pain of her bloodied nose. It was still dripping, and there was blood on her cloak and on her fingers. 'I'm not leaving her here like she's rubbish. Come on. Help me.' She started to gather up the shards of glass, piling them in Eliza's velvet cloak.

After a moment or so, Mariana began to help her. In the darkening evening, it was almost impossible to find the smaller pieces of glass, and they were working half by feel, flinching away from the sharp edges. Mariana caught her breath as she sliced her finger, and then began to cry, the small pain suddenly unbearable.

'Oh, don't!' Julia flung her arms around her. 'Don't. We have to find the pieces, we can't leave even one tiny bit behind. Perhaps your father would be able to mend her?'

'I don't think so.' Mariana shook her head. 'It was Eliza's own breath that made her real, instead of just a pretty toy. It's all gone now, it must be.' Her breath hitched in her throat. 'She's just floated away into the air.'

She stirred the glass fragments in the cloak, mixed up with scraps of silk from Eliza's pretty lilac dress. There were no pieces of purple glass from the bubble of Eliza's breath. Were there? What if there was a chance, and she missed it? She couldn't see for tears. 'I need a light,' she whispered huskily. 'I can't see. You're right. We can't leave any of her behind.'

She picked up a long shard and started to scratch on the stones with it, drawing the shape of a lantern as well as she could by feel, brushing away the drops of blood from her cut hand with impatient misery.

The lantern came to life slowly, a soft glow rising out of the stones, shedding its light on Mariana's tear-stained face, and the streaks of blood all over Julia's clothes.

Mariana sniffed. 'I can't take you back to the palazzo like that. I'll lose my place for sure.'

'I don't want to go back without her,' Julia said, her voice shaking. 'Are there any more pieces, now that you can see?'

'No… But there should be.' Mariana lifted up the lantern, looking around. 'There should be a purple glass ball – that was how my father made her live, it held Eliza's last breath inside it. I can't see it.' She sighed. 'I suppose the pieces are just too small to find.'

'Mariana.' Julia's voice was shaking. 'Look… Look at the lantern.'

Mariana glanced up at it. She hadn't bothered before; it was only there to help her find the last scraps of glass. She had assumed that there was a candle burning inside. That was what she had drawn, wasn't it?

What she held now was no simple candle lantern. The frame that held the glass panels was cast from some fine, silvery metal, with a delicate design of children running around the outside – three children, the littlest Eliza's size, then Julia chasing after her, and Mariana last, reaching out her hands to catch them. On the top of the lantern was the cat from the Renigo coat of arms, its tail curled over into a loop for hanging.

But it was the light that Mariana and Julia were staring at. Through the glass panels came a clear violet glow – the colour of Signor Nesso's berry-scented tonic, the colour of the glass bubble. Eliza's colour.

'Is it her?' Julia clutched at Mariana's arm. 'Is she there?'

'I – I don't know. Oh!' For the merest second, a child's face had appeared in the purple light, a little smiling girl, looking out at them – laughing.

'It is! It is!' Julia squeaked.

'I didn't know that was what I was doing,' Mariana said wonderingly. 'I wanted a lantern…'

'You *wanted* Eliza back,' Julia pointed out. 'You got them both together. All the glass pieces are gone, look.' She held up the empty cloak.

'Eliza didn't come back just for me.' Mariana ran her finger over the three children moulded in the silver framework of the lantern. 'You, too.' She shivered a little. 'It's part of each of us.'

'How? Because we were both wishing for her back?'

'Yes – but truly part of us too. The blood from my cut fingers, and your nose, where my stepmother hit you.'

'Then is Eliza a little bit my sister now too?' Julia whispered, her eyes shining with hope in the lantern-light.

A tiny hand appeared in the light, pressed up against the glass, and both girls reached for it, resting their palms together against Eliza's on the other side.

'Yes.' Mariana closed her hand around Julia's. 'She belongs to us both.'

LATER

MARIANA DIPPED HER QUILL PEN in the ink bottle, and rested her chin on her hand. She was supposed to be sketching leaves. Signor Felsi, the painter, wanted her to improve the accuracy of her drawing. He and Signor Nesso had designed her lessons together, since her magic seemed to be so tightly bound up with her drawing. She had learned a few simple spells from Signor Nesso, but it was in the drawn magic that her real power showed through.

Somehow, though, leaves were not what she

wanted to draw. She found herself sketching faces instead. Julia. Leo. The count. Even her stepmother's wide, blank eyes appeared under her pen. Mariana shuddered. After a few weeks of studying, she knew a little more about the magic now, and how to control it. She could draw without bringing her subjects to life, but the little faces seemed to watch her as she got up, and moved restlessly around the room.

Signor Nesso had hired carpenters to come in and work on the old rooms above the shop, to create a space for Mariana to sleep and study. He himself slept in the cubbyhole behind the velvet curtain, and used the rest of the space for more bags and boxes and jars, and the strange curios he had picked up in a lifetime of magic.

She went to the heavy folder of drawings, lying propped up against the wall, and undid the ribbons at the top so that she could leaf through the pages. She flicked past the different studies Signor Felsi had set her to make, until she came to a smaller piece of thick, heavy paper, softened at the edges by much handling.

She looked at it almost every day, perhaps adding a line or two here and there, waiting for the day when it would be finished, and her magic would be strong enough to make it real again.

The girl of glass stared back at her from the paper, and Mariana pressed the drawing close, remembering her sister's cool glass cheek against her own.

Have you read the first enchanting
story from Magical Venice? * *

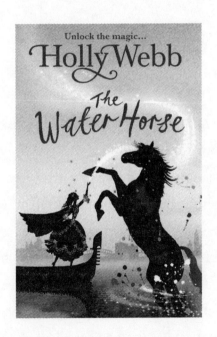

Read on for a sneak peek…

CHAPTER ONE

THE GIRL IN THE KINGFISHER blue dress dipped and swirled and spun across the floor, with the young boy laughing and twirling after her. Her mask was a glittering bird, to match her feathered dress, and his was a fox, sharp-nosed, with silver wire whiskers. He didn't know who she was, but he had asked her to dance after he saw her swipe a fingerful of cream from the top of one of the elaborate trifles on the supper table. She had seen him watching, and she'd looked so guilty, even under the mask, that he'd laughed out loud, and she had laughed too.

'Shall we dance the next one?' he asked her eagerly, and brushed a kiss across her hand.

But then her dark eyes behind the mask clouded, and she muttered an excuse and hurried away, leaving him standing in the middle of the floor.

Had he offended her, asking for another dance? He watched her dart through the crowds and away into another room and sighed. He would go and wait by the supper table, to see if she came back.

But the girl in the kingfisher dress had flung herself through the laughing, dancing partygoers to a discreet little side-room. It was reserved for ladies who found themselves caught short, and needed help with their hundred-layered petticoats, and stiff satin skirts. She shut the door, and leaned on it, wishing she hadn't let that boy swing her round and round so fast. All that cream, on top of crystallised fruits. She should have been more careful. It was just so exciting not to be a princess, for a night. Everyone wore masks on New Year's Eve, it was the tradition, and Venice was a city that lived by its traditions.

If he'd known who she was, he would have treated her like the blown glass from the islands. He wouldn't even have dared to touch her hand – let alone kiss it.

The young servant girl left in charge of the room didn't recognise Olivia for the princess either, not in her jewelled bird mask, topped with its crown of gleaming feathers. There were several other little birds dancing in the halls, and the girl dipped a sketchy curtsey, and smirked as Olivia snatched at a basin, and sank into a chair, gulping painfully. It was no good. She fought at the ribbon ties and tore off her mask to be quietly sick.

Then she caught the maid's eye as she looked up, and saw the expressions flit across the girl's face. Shock. Fear that she had been rude. And was that excitement, just a little, at being so close to the princess?

But mostly there was a sharp, undisguised look of dislike.

Why did the girl hate her so?

Olivia blinked, and the maid suddenly busied herself tidying away the basin, and fetching a delicate glass of cool water with lemon peel, and a bowl of warm water for the princess to wash her hands. She didn't look up at Olivia again.

The strangeness of that look hid what had happened for a moment, but as Olivia lay back in the chair and watched the girl scurry about, she realised that she felt quite odd. Not ill – this was a clearness in her head. A sharpness to her thoughts – perhaps it was why she had noticed the girl's angry face. Usually she wouldn't even have cared. She didn't look at servants, why would she?

As she patted her cheeks with a scented cloth, and dabbed perfume in the hollows of her neck, Olivia realised that everything felt different. Things were… brighter. It was the only way she could describe it – as if a layer of dust had been swept away. Pretty, glittery dust, but dust that had still softened and furred the edges of her thoughts.

A dust that had bewitched her since she was tiny.

A spell – lots of spells – floating away into the air like glittering dust motes. She had broken free, when she'd never even known that she was bound...

The water closed over her face, jade green, milky and warm, and she breathed bubbles. Her lungs burned, and she gasped in water, choking and struggling as the sunlight drifted further away...

'My lady?'

Warmth – a strong body, pushing her back up to the surface...

Someone was standing outside the thick, embroidered curtains and whispering. They were only whispering very, very quietly, of course. It would be most improper for anyone to raise their voice to the daughter of the duke.

Olivia surfaced slowly, dragging herself from deep, watery dreams. She stretched out a pale hand, wafting it vaguely at the heavy brocade. At once, the maid drew the curtains aside. She looked relieved, Olivia thought, trying not to smile.